S0-BOL-183

THE SHEIKH'S
DESTINY

THE SHEIKH'S DESTINY

BY

MELISSA JAMES

NEW HANOVER COUNTY
PUBLIC LIBRARY
201 CHESTNUT STREET
WILMINGTON, NC 28401

All the characters in this book have no existence outside the imagination of the author, and have no relation whatsoever to anyone bearing the same name or names. They are not even distantly inspired by any individual known or unknown to the author, and all the incidents are pure invention.

All Rights Reserved including the right of reproduction in whole or in part in any form. This edition is published by arrangement with Harlequin Enterprises II BV/S.à.r.l. The text of this publication or any part thereof may not be reproduced or transmitted in any form or by any means, electronic or mechanical, including photocopying, recording, storage in an information retrieval system, or otherwise, without the written permission of the publisher.

® and TM are trademarks owned and used by the trademark owner and/or its licensee. Trademarks marked with ® are registered with the United Kingdom Patent Office and/or the Office for Harmonisation in the Internal Market and in other countries.

First published in Great Britain 2010
Large Print edition 2010
Harlequin Mills & Boon Limited,
Eton House, 18-24 Paradise Road,
Richmond, Surrey TW9 1SR

© Lisa Chaplin 2010

ISBN: 978 0 263 21259 4

Harlequin Mills & Boon policy is to use papers that are natural, renewable and recyclable products and made from wood grown in sustainable forests. The logging and manufacturing process conform to the legal environmental regulations of the country of origin.

Printed and bound in Great Britain
by CPI Antony Rowe, Chippenham, Wiltshire

This book is dedicated to Vicky,
my beloved sister-in-law, who never once denigrated
this job I love, and despite dyslexia bought and read
every book I've had released. To a wonderful sister
and dearly beloved aunt to my kids, thank you for
showing us what true courage under fire means.
We think of you and miss you every day.
2nd December 1963–9th October 2009

To Michelle, Donna and Lisa,
the "angels" who nursed Vicky through her illness,
giving her last months dignity and love despite
work and family commitments. Thank you from
the bottom of my heart. I can only invent heroines—
but each of you is one in the eyes of our family,
and all the many who loved Vicky.

PROLOGUE

The road to Shellah-Akbar, Northern Africa

THEY were closing in on him. Time to open throttle.

Alim El-Kanar shifted down into low-gear sports mode, in the truck he'd modified specially for this purpose. He wasn't letting the men of the warlord Sh'ellah—after whose family this region had been named—take the medical supplies and food meant for those the man made suffer, so he could keep control and live in luxury. Alim wasn't going to be caught, either—that would be disaster, but for the people of this region, not him. As soon as Sh'ellah saw the face of the man he'd taken hostage, he'd hold Alim for a fabulous ransom that would keep them in funds for new weapons for years.

When he had the ransom, *then* he'd kill him— if he could get away with it.

But Sh'ellah hadn't yet discovered who Alim

was, and he gambled his life on the hope the warlord never would. Even the director of Doctors for Africa didn't know the true identity of the near-silent truck driver who pulled off what he called miracles on a regular basis, reaching remote villages held by warlords with medicine, food and water-purifying tablets.

With a top-class fake ID and always wearing the male headscarf he could twist over his famous features whenever he chose, he was invisible to the world. Just the way he liked it.

Who he was—or what he'd been once—mattered far less than what he did.

He always gave enough medicine to each village to last six to eight hours. Then, when Sh'ellah's men came for their 'share', most of it was gone; they took a few needles, some out-of-date antibiotics, and strutted out again.

The villagers never told Alim where they hid the supplies, and he didn't want to know. They kept just enough bread, rice and grain out for Sh'ellah's men to feel smug about their theft. To Sh'ellah, such petty control made him feel like a man, a lion among mice.

Even Alim, flawed as he was, would be a better leader—

Don't go there. Grimly he shifted down gear, following the indented tracks in the scrubby grass on what was loosely called a road to the village of Shellah-Akbar. He'd had tyres put on this truck like the ones used in outback and desert rallies so he could fly over rocks and sudden holes the wind made in the dusty ground. He also had a padded protective cage put inside the cab, much like the one he'd had in his cars when he was still The Racing Sheikh.

He'd once been so ridiculously proud of the nickname—now he wanted to hit something every time he thought of it. His fame and life in the fast lane had died the same day as his brother. The only racing he did now was with trucks with much needed supplies to war-torn villages. And if the term 'sheikh' was technically correct, it was a privilege he'd forfeited after Fadi's death. It was an honour he'd never deserve. His younger brother Harun had taken on the honour in his absence, marrying the princess Fadi had been contracted to marry. Harun had been ruling the people of his principality, Abbas al-Din—*the lion of the faith*—for three years, and was doing a brilliant job.

Thinking of home set off the familiar ache. He

used to love coming home. *Habib Abbas*, the people would chant. *Beloved lion*. They'd been so proud of his achievements.

If the people wanted him to come home, to take his place among his people, he knew an accident of birth, finding some oil or minerals, or the ability to race a car around a track didn't make a true leader. Strength, good sense and courage did—and Alim had lost the best of those qualities with Fadi's death, along with his heart and a lot of his skin. He had just enough strength and courage left to risk his neck for a few villagers in Africa. The fanfare for what he did was silent, and that was the way he liked it.

He growled as his usual stress-trigger, the puckered scars that covered more than half his torso, began the painful itching that scratching only made worse. He'd have to use the last of his silica-based cream on the pain as soon as he had a minute, as soon as he lost these jokers—and he would. He wasn't Habib Abbas, or The Racing Sheikh, any more—but he still had the skills.

Stop it! Thinking only made the itch worse—and the heart-pain that was his night-and-day companion. *Fadi, I'm so sorry!*

Grimly he turned his mind to the job at hand,

or he'd crash in seconds. The protective roll cage inside his truck might be heavily padded with lamb's wool so if the truck rolled, he could use his modified low centre of gravity shift and oddly placed air bags to flip back right way up—but it wouldn't help if he was too busted up to keep going.

He checked the mirror. They were still the same distance behind him, forty men packing weaponry suitable for taking far more than a truck. They were too far away from him to shoot accurately, but still too close to shake. He couldn't do anything clever on this rugged, roadless terrain, like spilling oil to make them slide: it would sink straight into the dirt before the enemy reached the slick, and he'd risk his engine for nothing.

But he had to do something, or they'd follow him right to Shellah-Akbar and take the supplies. He had to find a way to beat the odds currently stacked against him like the Spartans at Thermopylae thousands of years ago.

If he could rig something with the emergency flare…could he make it work?

Alim's mind raced. Yes, if he added the tar-based chemical powder he kept to help the tyres move over the sand without sliding to the volatile formula inside the flare, and tossed it back, it might work—

He was used to driving one-handed, or steering the wheel with both feet. He shoved a stone on the accelerator, angling it so it kept going steady, and drove with his feet while pulling the flare apart with as much care as he could, given his situation.

He was nearing the four-way junction ten miles from the village, where he must turn one way or another. He had to stop them now or, no matter what clever methods he employed to evade them, they'd know where he was going. They'd use their satellite phones, and another hundred thugs would be at the village before sunset, demanding their 'rightful' share of the supplies proven by their assault rifles.

He poured the powder in with shaking hands. He had to be careful or he'd kill them; and, murderers though most of the men undoubtedly were, it wasn't his place to judge who had done what or why. He'd had a childhood of extreme privilege, the best education in the world. Most of the men behind him had been born in horrendous poverty, abducted when they were small children and taught to play with AK-47s instead of bats and balls.

He'd leave enough food and supplies behind so their warlord didn't kill them for their failure. Part of the solution or perpetuating the problem, he didn't know; but in this continent where human life was cheaper than clean water, everyone only had one shot at living, and he refused to carry any more regrets in his personal backpack.

He grabbed the wheel as he neared the far-leaning sign showing the way to the villages, and slanted the truck extreme left, away from all of them. Good, the wind was shifting again: it was time for a good old-fashioned wild goose chase.

He put the flare together, closing it tight with electrical tape, shook it and opened the sunroof. He lit the flare, counted one-hundred-and-one to one-hundred-and-seven, shoved his foot hard over the stone covering the accelerator as he tossed the lit flare up and backward, and pulled the sunroof shut.

The truck shot forward and left, when the *boom* and flash came. The air behind him turned a dazzling bluish-white, then thick and black, filled with choking, temporarily blinding chemicals. Screams came to his ears, the screeches of tyres as their Jeeps came to simultaneous halts. He'd done it… Alim arced the truck hard right, back to the crossroads. He didn't wind down the window to check. He'd either blinded them all, or he'd be dead inside a minute.

Half a kilometre before the junction, he threw out the half-dozen boxes of second-rate supplies he'd been keeping for the warlord's pleasure. They'd find them when the chemical reaction from their tears would neutralise the blindness. There was no permanent damage to their retinas, only to their pride and their ability to follow him for about half an hour. Factoring in the wind shift, all traces of his tyre tracks should have vanished by then, covered with red earth and falling leaves and branches from the low, thin trees. They'd have to split up to find him, and by the time they reached the village he'd be long gone.

Then a whining sound came; air whooshed, a loud *bang* filled the cab, and the truck leaped forward as if propelled before it teetered and fell to the left.

Alim's head struck the side window with stunning force. Blood filled his eye; he felt his mind reeling. One of his specially made, ultra-wide and thick desert tyres had blown. One of the warlord's men was either not blinded in the explosion, or he'd made the luckiest shot in the world, and blown his back tyre. The only drawback to his special, extra-tough tyres was their need for perfect balance. If one tyre went, so did the truck.

He couldn't black out now, or he'd die—and so would the people of Shellah-Akbar. He fought passing out with everything in him. He stopped the truck and pulled on the air-bag lever. As the truck tipped, the four-foot-thick pillows that flew to position outside the doors bounced it back up. As the truck righted itself he took his rifle and blew the tyres, the two on the passenger side quickly, but he had to wait until the truck was up and keeling back over to the right before he could balance it by blowing the driver's side.

The truck landed hard down on the ground as the blackness took over. Alim shoved the truck in first and took off. The rocks and sand would destroy the thick rubber coating with which he'd covered his rims in case of emergency, but he could make far more than the remaining six miles, and there were spare tyres in the back. The tyres weren't modified, and it'd be a miracle if he made it back to the Human Compassion Refugee camp two hundred and sixty kilometres south-west, but it would get him to where the food-aid pilots could pick him up.

He had to reach the village; he was going to pass out any moment. Blood gushed from his temple wound, and his blood pressure was falling by the second. If he could put the truck in the right direction, and set the cruise control…the compass and GPS system both said he only needed a straight line now to make it.

He pressed the emergency direction finder on his satellite phone; his only hope now was that the nurse he knew lived in Shellah-Akbar had her receiver switched on.

Holding the wheel like grim death, he put the truck in second, made sure the stone was still in place over the accelerator, and fell forward.

The truck came into the village of Shellah-Akbar seventeen minutes later.

A woman was at the wheel. She'd run from her bunk in the medical tent as soon as the emergency signal reached the village. The only one with full medical experience, she'd ridden an old bike as fast as she could while Abdel, the village Olympic marathon hopeful, followed, to ride the pushbike back to the village. While the truck was still moving she'd stopped just in front of the driver's door, tossed the bike down for Abdel to find, yanked open the door and jumped inside. Sprawled beside her, his head in her lap, was one unconscious driver, who had risked his life so that others may live.

'*In-sh'allah,*' she whispered, and recited the words of a prayer taught her from infancy: a prayer that hadn't kept her own life intact, but might help God smile upon this courageous man.

He wasn't going to die. Not today. Not if she could help it.

CHAPTER ONE

'GET the driver into my hut, and get rid of the truck,' Hana al-Sud yelled to two villagers in Swahili when she pulled the truck up outside the medical tent. 'Don't cook the food. Feed plain bread to those who need it most. Bury the rest in Saliya's grave.'

'The fruit will lose its vitamins, Hana,' her assistant protested.

'One seed or core can be found in seconds,' she replied calmly enough, given the urgency of their situation and the rapid pounding of her heart. She ran around the truck to the driver. 'We can get it back out tonight to feed the children, without losing nutritional value. Just do it, please, Malika! And sweep away any traces of tyre marks!'

An older man ran to the passenger side to take the driver as the fittest young man in the village

jumped into Hana's place in the driver's seat.
The other villagers opened the back of the truck
to unload it. Two women ran over with the vital
tarpaulins, snatched medical kits and ampoules
of antibiotics and insulin to bury it. The future of
the entire village depended on everyone working
together, and working fast. They'd be here in
minutes. The warlord's satellite phones were the
best money could buy. Any sniff of betrayal
meant unbearable consequences for them all.

'Take the driver to my hut. He's Arabic,' Hana
said tensely in Swahili. 'I'll patch him up. When
they ask I'll say my husband came for me.'

The men took the unconscious man to Hana's
small hut beside the medical tent.

Within fifteen minutes it was as if the truck had
never been there. Abdel would leave it somewhere in the desert, take the exact coordinates
and return on foot. He was the only one with the
perfect cover. As he was a long-distance runner
aiming for the Olympics, no one thought it
strange if he wasn't in the village at all times.

In the hut, Hana had the injured man laid on
an old sheet. 'Wound and suture kit—an old re-
sterilised set.' This brave man deserved better,
but if she used the new kits he'd brought today

and didn't dispose of them in time, the warlord's men would know the truth. They had to get every detail right.

There was blood on his face and shirt. 'Haytham, I need a clean shirt!' Haytham was her friend Malika's husband, and approximately the same size as this man. She stripped off the bloodied shirt and tossed it in her cooking fire, noting the angry, inflamed mass of burns scars criss-crossing his chest, shoulder and stomach on the left side. She'd treat them later. Right now she had to save his life.

She checked her watch. From experience, she knew she had five minutes to get it all done. She cleaned his face of the blood, and prepared to suture the wound. She'd wash his hair after, to remove the last traces of his identity as the driver.

She stitched his wound as fast as she could, grateful it was close to his hair; she'd cover it with his fringe, and would have to risk infection by using cover-stick around the reddened skin. There was no way she could risk a bandage, but she'd use one vital ampoule of antibiotic, needle and syringe; the wound could turn septic with hair and make-up on it.

She injected him between his toes, as if he were

a junkie with collapsed veins. It was a place Sh'ellah's men wouldn't think to look for signs of injury and medical attention. 'Bury these fast,' she ordered Malika, who took the precious supplies and ran.

Hana washed the worst of the dirt and blood from his hair with a damp washer, coated with some of her precious essential oils, and covered the wound with the cleaned hair and make-up. Then she rolled the man off the sheet, bundled it up and tossed it in the roaring fire. She put the clean shirt on him—he'd been through several operations for those burns, by the patches of grafted skin over the worst of it—buttoned up the shirt, and checked her watch. Four minutes thirty-eight. Not bad, really. She checked over the hut for any signs of wound treatment.

Nothing, thank God. Hana dragged in a deep sigh of relief, and finally allowed herself a moment to look at her patient's face.

'*No, no,*' she whispered, horrified.

She'd known as she ran to save this man's life that he'd pulled off the impossible today—but the feat suddenly didn't seem quite so impossible, if he was who she thought he was.

Please, God, just make it a freak physical re-

semblance…because if it was him, then by his mere presence he'd brought far more danger to the village than by any supplies he'd brought.

Even Sh'ellah's followers would know him. Most men loved fast sports and money, and this man combined both. Just put a helmet on him and it was the former face of the world's most expensive racing-car team. He'd won the World Championship twice—and brought both riches and research to a once-struggling nation. He'd found oil and natural gas reserves in a place few had thought to look, with his chemical background and analytical racing driver's mind.

'*La!*' he muttered, in either fever or concussed confusion. '*La, la, akh! Fadi, la!*'

No, no, brother! Fadi, no!

In dread, Hana heard the words in the Arabic native to her childhood home country, begging his beloved brother Fadi to live. It broke her heart—she knew how it felt to lose those she loved—and then she listened in horror as he relived the drive to the village in graphic detail, including the complex mixture of chemicals he'd used to blind Sh'ellah's men.

The fine-chiselled, handsome face—the faint scars of burns on his cheek, the horrific wounds on his body…even his miraculous escape today made perfect sense. He'd obviously had extensive training in the creation of compounds, and how much of each to add to make something new—such as a flare that could blind the men chasing him.

'This is all I need,' she muttered in frustration to the delirious face of Alim El-Kanar, the missing sheikh of Abbas al-Din. 'Why couldn't you be anywhere but here?'

The former racing-car champion kept muttering, describing the flare-bomb he'd made.

At the worst possible moment, the sound of a dozen all-terrain vehicles bumping hard and fast over the non-existent road reached her. Sh'ellah's men all spoke Arabic similar to that of the man lying in front of her. They'd identify him in moments, take him for enormous ransom…and destroy any evidence of their abduction. Within ten minutes she and all her friends would be blown to bits: another statistic to a world so inured to violence that they'd be lucky to make it to page twenty of a newspaper, or on the TV behind some Hollywood star's latest drunken tantrum.

'Fadi—Fadi, please, stay with me, brother! Stay!'

She had to do it. With a silent apology to the hero of her village, she heated a wet cloth over the fire and shoved it over his famous features to accelerate the fever already beginning to burn under his skin; she rubbed him down with a dry towel to make the temperature of his arms and legs rise. Her only chance lay with scaring the men into staying away from him…

And by shutting him up. She put her fingers to his throat and pushed down on his carotid artery, counting a slow, agonising one to twenty, until he collapsed into unconsciousness.

He had to be dreaming, but it was the sweetest dream of angel eyes.

Alim felt the fever creating needle-pricks of pain beneath his skin, the throbbing pain at his temple…but as he opened his eyes the confusion grew. Surely he was in Africa still? The hut looked African enough with its unglazed windows, and the cooking fire in the centre of the single room; the heat and dust, red dirt not sand, told him he was still in the Dark Continent.

'Where am I?' he asked the veiled woman bending over the cooking fire.

When she turned and limped towards him, he

recognised the vortex of his centrifugal confusion: his angel-eyed goddess wasn't African. The face bending to his was half covered with a veil, but the green-brown eyes that weren't quite looking in his, gently slanted and surrounded by glowing olive skin, were definitely Arabic. They were so beautiful, and reminded him so much of home, he ached in places she hadn't disinfected or stitched up.

Perhaps it was the limp—anyone who climbed into a moving truck would have to hurt themselves; or maybe it was her voice he'd heard in fevered sleep, begging him to be quiet—but he was certain she'd been the one to save his life.

'You're in the village of Shellah-Akbar. How are you feeling?' she asked in Maghreb Arabic, a North African dialect related to his native tongue—haunting him with the familiarity. She was from his region—though she had the strangest accent, an unusual twang. He couldn't place it.

Intrigued, he said, 'I'm well, thank you,' in Gulf Arabic. His voice was rough against the symphony of hers, like a tiger sitting at the feet of a nightingale.

Her lashes fluttered down, but not in a flirta-
tious way; she acted like the shyest virgin in his
home city. But she was veiled as a married
woman, and working here as the nurse. He remembered her rapping out orders to others in
several languages, including Swahili.

His saviour with the angel eyes was a modern
woman, too confident in her orders and sure of
her place to be single. Yet she chose to remain
veiled, and she wouldn't meet his eyes.

She must be married to a doctor here. That
had to be it.

It had been so long since he'd seen a woman
behave in this manner he'd almost forgotten its
tender reassurance: faithful women did exist. It
had been a rare commodity in the racing world,
and he'd seen few women that intrigued him in
any manner since the accident.

'Now could you please tell me the truth?'

The semi-stringent demand made his dreams
of gentle, angel-eyed maidens drop and quietly
shatter. He looked up, saw her frowning as she
inspected his wound. 'It's infected,' she
muttered, probing with butterfly fingers. He
breathed in the scent of woman and lavender, a
combination that somehow touched him deep

inside. 'I'm sorry. I had to cover the sutures with make-up and your hair, and increase your fever so Sh'ellah's men would believe you had the flu.'

'I've had far worse.' He saw the self-recrimination in those lovely eyes, heard it in the soft music of her voice. Wanting to see her shine again, he murmured, 'You were the one who came to the truck. That's why you're limping.'

Slowly she nodded, but the shadows remained.

'Did you stitch me up?'

Another nod, curt and filled with self-anger. Strange, but he could almost hear her thoughts, the emotions she tried to hide. It was as if something inside her were singing to him in silence, crying out to be understood.

Perhaps she was as isolated, as lonely for her people as he was. Why was she here?

'May I know my saviour's name?' he asked, his tone neutral, holding none of the strange tenderness she evoked in him.

The hesitation was palpable, the indecision. He took pity on her. 'If your husband…'

'I have no husband.' Her words had lost their music; they were curt and cold. She turned from him; moments later he heard the tearing sound of a medical pack opening.

He closed his eyes, cursing himself for not understanding in the first place. It had been so long since he'd dealt with a woman of his faith he'd almost forgotten: only a widow would come here, and one without a family to protect her. So young for such a loss. 'I'm sorry.'

With a little half-shrug, she leaned down to his wound. 'Please lie still. If your wound is to heal—and it has to do that, fast, before Sh'ellah's men return—I have to clean it again.'

He should have known she wouldn't be working on a man in this manner if she was married, unless she'd been married to a Westerner, and then she wouldn't be veiled.

The veil suited her, though. The seductive sweep of the sand-hued material over her face and body covered her form in comfort but protected her skin from the stinging dirt and winds without binding her. And the soft swish of the hand-stitched material as she walked—how she moved so beautifully with a limp was unfathomable, but he knew his angel was also his saviour.

She walks in beauty like the night. Or like a star of the sunrise…

'Thank you for saving my worthless life, Sahar Thurayya,' he said, with a bowing motion of his hands, since he couldn't move his head without ruining her work.

A brow lifted at the title he'd given her, *dawn star*, a courtesy name since she refused to give him her true name, but she continued her work without speaking.

'My name is Alim.'

To give her that much truth was safe. There were many men named Alim in his country, and courtesy demanded she introduce herself in return.

'Though dawn star is prettier,' she said quietly, 'my name is Hana.'

Hana meant *happiness*. 'I think *dawn star* is more suited to the woman you've become.'

She didn't look up from the intricate task of cleaning hair and packed-on make-up from his wound. 'You've known me all of ten minutes, yet you feel qualified to make such a judgement?'

She was right. Just because she was here, cut off from her own people, and was radiant with all forms of beauty *but* happiness—she seemed haunted somehow—gave him no right to judge her. 'I beg your pardon,' he said gravely in the dialect of his homeland.

'Please stop talking,' she whispered.

It was only then that he noticed the fine tremors

in her hand. So his mere presence, their shared language, hurt her heart as much as hers did him. He closed his eyes and let her work in peace, breathing in the clean warm air and scent of lavender, a natural disinfectant.

She still wasn't risking using the medicines he'd brought, then.

When she seemed to be almost done with his wound, he murmured, 'Where's my truck?'

'Abdel drove it out to a remote part of the area. The villagers wiped all traces of the tyre tracks from the way in and out of the village. Don't worry, he'll hide it well, and will give you exact coordinates so you can get to it when you're feeling better.'

'Who am I?' When she frowned at him, obviously wondering if concussion had given him temporary amnesia, he added, 'To Sh'ellah's men, when they came? Who did you say I was?'

The fingers placing Steri-Strips over his wound trembled for a moment; again her agony of indecision felt like shimmering heat rising in waves from her skin.

He waited in silence. It seemed the last thing she needed was his voice, his language and accent reminding her of what she no longer had—though he wondered why she wasn't home with their people. Why his presence hurt her so.

She put the last Steri-Strip over his wound, and stepped back. 'When they came, I wore a full burq'a so they'd assume I was married. If they can't see, there's less for them to be tempted. You know how life is here.'

Intrigued again by this woman and the most prosaic acceptance of the ugly side of life, he nodded.

'When they came in here, they assumed you were my husband. Even unconscious, your presence as my man inspired respect for me, and protected me from abduction and rape—for now at least,' she finished bluntly. 'Sh'ellah still wants us to believe he's our saviour, and we're not giving him any reason to think otherwise.'

Alim saw the bubbling mass of emotion inside her pull apart into distinct, jagged pieces. Memory began returning to him like little shards of glass. She'd risked her life to come to him in the truck; she'd done so again by treating him in her hut, and claiming him as her man. He owed this woman his life at least twice over.

Slowly, as delicately as if he were creating an explosive cocktail of chemicals, he said, 'I'm privileged to be your husband in name, Sahar Thurayya. I'd be more honoured still if you would trust me while I'm here. It won't be long.'

She returned to his bedside with a cup of water. She took a sip first, then handed it to him and he drank in turn, his eyes on hers. The cup of agreement and peace: a traditional sign of mutual respect. A tradition he'd once given and accepted with so little thought—but now, looking in those brave, sad eyes, he felt the full honour of her offer.

It told him far more about this woman than anything that had come from her mouth. She was from Abbas al-Din, no matter what language she spoke.

Her eyes smiled, but her hand didn't touch his as she gave him the cup. 'Thank you.'

He noted she didn't use his name; she still kept her distance. In Hana's eyes, obviously trust was something earned, not given. He wondered how high the cost had been for misplaced trust in the past. Why did a woman with such pain beneath her smile risk her life and virtue in a place where nobody would live, if they had a choice?

'I'm afraid you can't leave yet. They know the supplies went somewhere, and you're the only stranger in the district,' she said as he filled his parched throat with cool water. 'Sh'ellah will have placed a dozen men on every way out of the village. They've been here several times in past months, collecting more than half our millet and corn harvest to feed his soldiers,' she said, bitterness threading through her voice. 'With a stranger in the village, they'll be watching all of us for weeks to come.' She sounded strained as she added, 'So I'm glad of your promise, since we will have to share my hut as husband and wife. There's only one bed here.'

He choked on the final gulp of liquid. Coughing, he turned his gaze to her. Strange that, with a throbbing headache and eyes stinging, he knew where she was at all times. His ears strained for the swish of her burq'a. She made a sound he'd heard all his life so alluring, so incredibly feminine. She seemed to infuse her every movement with life, light and beauty.

She made a sound of distress as she went on, 'I'm sorry, but we can't afford to bring in a spare bed in case Sh'ellah's men raid during the night, or lead a sneak attack. We have to sleep in one bed or risk suspicion—and out here suspicion is explained with an assault rifle.'

Alim stared at her back, so unyielding, refusing

to face him. He thought of every day of his adult life spent avoiding this kind of intimacy, using the death of his young wife ten years before—the wife he'd liked but had never loved—as his excuse not to fulfil his duty and remarry. He thought of his adopted career of car racing, travelling from place to place, never settling down—holding himself off from living. Even now, wasn't he in hiding?

And he smiled; he grinned, and then burst out laughing.

'What's so funny?' Hana turned on him at the first sound of the chuckle bursting from his lips. Her veil fell from her lower face, showing lush dusky lips pursed with indignation. Her eyes flashed; even in the midst of angry demand, her voice was like the music of a waterfall. Her face, now revealed for a moment in all its glory, was harmony to its symphony.

And he was a complete idiot to think of her that way.

But it was the first time he'd truly laughed in three years, and he found that once he started again, he couldn't stop. 'It's—it's so absurd,' he gasped between fresh gusts of mirth.

Hana straightened her shoulders and looked

him right in the eyes for the first time—and hers were contemptuous. Every feature of that lovely face showed disdain. 'Maybe it's ridiculous to you, but if it saves the lives of a hundred people—and I presume you care about their lives, since you risked your life to come here with food and medicines for them—I'll put up with the absurdity. The question is, will you?'

CHAPTER TWO

'WHAT'S the unusual note in your accent?' the sheikh asked her, his tone abrupt at the subject change, but his dark green eyes were curious. Assessing her beyond the questions his simple words spoke. 'You haven't lived in the emirates all your life.'

Hana felt as if he were dissecting her without a scalpel. So he hadn't been fooled by her use of Maghreb, nor put off by her unaccustomed abruptness.

Not in the six months she'd been here in the village had simple conversation been fraught with such danger. If he knew the truth about his so-called saviour, he could take her freedom away with a snap of his fingers.

Her heart beat faster at the thought of saying anything—but thousands of Arabic girls grew up in Australia. Not so many people from Abbas al-Din had lived in Perth, of course, but enough that she wouldn't be easily traced.

Then she laughed at herself. What a ridiculous thought—as if Alim El-Kanar would care enough to trace her past! This wasn't the kind of information she needed to hide; it wasn't the reason she'd been shunned by her people. 'I was born in the emirates, but raised in Australia from the age of seven,' she answered, realising that a few minutes had passed while she'd been lost in thought—and that he'd allowed her to think without interruption.

'Ah.' He relaxed back on his pillows; she'd barely noticed his tension until then. 'I couldn't place the twang. Are you fluent in English?' he asked, changing languages without a break in speaking.

She nodded, answering in English. 'I lived there from the ages of seven to twenty-one, and went to state-run English schools.'

He grinned. 'You sound totally Aussie now you're speaking English.'

She laughed. 'I guess that's how I consider myself, mostly. My dad—' she'd practised so long, she could say 'dad' without choking up any more '—was offered an opportunity in the mining industry. He was a miner, but saved enough to go to university, and became an engineer. So he was rather unique in that he knew both sides…' *And that was way too much infor-mation!* She clamped her lips shut.

'I can see why any big mining corporation would want him,' he said, sounding thoughtful.

She'd started this, she had to finish or the sheikh would remember the conversation long after he was gone. She forced a smile through the lump in her throat, 'Yes, the money he was offered was so large he felt it would be irrespon-sible to the family to not take it. When we'd been there a little while, he and Mum felt it would be best for us if we retained our culture, but under-stood and respected the one we lived in. We lived not far from other Arabic families—but while we attended Islamic lessons, we also attended local schools.' And she'd just said more words together about herself than she had in years. She closed her mouth.

After a slow, thoughtful pause, the sheikh— she couldn't help but think of him as that—said, 'So if your father was in the mining industry, you lived in the outback? Kalgoorlie or Tom Price, or maybe the Kimberley Ranges?'

Her pulse pounded in her throat until her breath

laboured. 'No, we didn't, but he did. We—my mother, my sisters and brother and I—lived in a suburb of Perth, and Dad lived in Kalgoorlie and came home Fridays. He wanted us to live close to…amenities.'

The sheikh nodded. She saw it in his eyes: he'd noticed the omission of the word *mosque*.

Even thinking the word was painful. She couldn't enter a mosque without people wanting to know who she was and where she was from; and she couldn't lie. Not in a holy place.

So she didn't go any more.

'Did you always wear the burq'a?' he asked, with a gentle politeness that told her he respected her secrets, her right to not answer.

'No. I'm from a moderate Sunni family. I wear it for protection.' She shrugged. 'Sh'ellah's very sweet to us—most of the time. But he could turn without warning.'

He's already sent men to ask if I have a man, or whether they can see whether I am young and pretty enough for his tastes.

She kept the shudder inside. Sh'ellah might be sixty-two, but he was a man of strong passions. Though he kept two wives, he had concubines in droves—and those were the women who pleased him. The others he discarded…and none of them ever came home.

Since she'd had the first warning of Sh'ellah's tastes, she'd kept the burq'a on as a knight's armour, wore her fake wedding ring like a talisman. She'd claimed her husband was travelling, and he'd soon be on his way here.

Her time here was over. Now she'd claimed the sheikh as her husband, Sh'ellah would expect her to leave with the sheikh when he went. Otherwise she'd become fair game. She had two backpacks packed and ready, hidden in the dirt beneath her hut, ready to disappear at a moment's notice, to head by foot to the nearest refugee camp if need be. It was two hundred and sixty kilometres away, but she knew how to find edible plants filled with juice, and collect dew from upturned leaves. With two or three canteens of water, some purification tablets, three dozen long-hidden energy bars and a compass, she could travel at night and make it in fourteen days.

She'd been used for a man's purposes once. She'd rather die than be used that way again.

The sheikh nodded, as if he understood what she'd left unsaid. Maybe he did, if he'd been in the Sahel long enough.

'Were you brought up in the emirates?' She turned to the pit fire as she asked, making an infusion of her precious stores of willow bark for his fever in a tiny hanging pot. If people were seen to be carrying things into this hut, Sh'ellah's men would be searching here in minutes. She'd give them no excuse to pay attention to her.

She didn't have to wonder if he noticed she'd lapsed into their native language; she saw the flickering of those dark eyes, and knew he was sizing her up like one of his chemical equations. He took long moments to answer. 'Yes.'

That was it. Flat and unemotional-sounding, a mirror-world of unhealed pain behind the thin wall of glass, ready to shatter at a touch. She spooned some of her infusion into a cracked plastic mug. 'I'm sorry I have no honey to sweeten this, but it will lessen your pain.'

She saw the surprise come and go in his face. He wasn't going to ask, and she wasn't going to volunteer why she minded her own business; but she knew he'd think about it. Why she asked nothing more, demanded no answers in return for hers. 'Drink it all.'

He nodded, and took the cup from her. His

fingers brushed hers, and she felt a tiny shiver run through her. 'You don't call me by my name.'

She drew a breath to conquer the tiny tremors in her hands. What was wrong with her? 'You're a stranger, older than me, and risked a lot to help our village. I was taught respect.'

'I'm barely ten years your senior. I gave you my name,' he said, and drained the cup. He held it back out to her with a face devoid of expression, but she sensed the challenge within. The dominant male used to winning with open weapons…and beneath lurked a hint of irritation. He didn't like her calling him older. She hid the smile.

'You gave your name, but it's my choice to use it or not.' She took the cup back, neither seeking nor avoiding the touch. Just as she neither sought nor avoided his eyes. It was a trick her mother had taught her. *Everything you give to a man he can refuse to return, Hana. So give as little as possible, even a glance, until you are certain what kind of man you face.*

It had been good advice—until she'd met Mukhtar.

'You don't like my name, Sahar Thurayya?'

She washed the cup and returned it to its hook

on the wall. Since she had no bench or cupboard, all things were either stacked on a box or hung on walls. 'I'm waiting to see if you live up to it.' She didn't comment on his poetic name for her, but a faint thrill ran through her every time she heard it. Just as she caught her breath when he smiled with his eyes, or laughed. And when he touched her… She closed her eyes and uttered a silent prayer. Four hours in this man's company, three of them when he'd been unconscious, and she was already in danger.

'So I must live up to my name?' Again she heard that rich chuckle in his voice. Without even turning around, she could see his face in her mind's eye, beautiful even in its damaged state, alight with the mirth that made him look as he had four years ago, and she knew she was standing in emotional quicksand. 'My brother always said I was misnamed.'

Alim: wise, learned.

She didn't ask in what ways he was unwise. He'd risked his life over and over for the thrill of racing and winning…

'It seems we were both misnamed,' he added, the laughter in his tone asking her to see the joke, as he had.

Hana: happiness.

I used to live up to my name, she thought wistfully. *When I was engaged to Latif, about to become his wife, then I was a happy woman.*

Then Latif's younger brother Mukhtar came into her life—and Latif showed her what her dreams of love and happiness were worth.

'I need to check on my other patients,' she said quietly. Checking to be certain her veil fully covered her, she walked with an unhurried step towards the medical tent—it hurt to rush since she had twisted her knee climbing into his truck—feeling his gaze follow her for as long as she was in sight.

Alim watched the doorway with views to the medical hut long after he could no longer see her. He still watched while the setting sun flooded the open door, long after his eyes hurt with the brightness and his head began knocking with the pain that would soon upgrade as the foul stuff she'd given him wore off.

She didn't draw attention to herself in any way—quite the opposite, including the burq'a the colour of sand, obviously handmade. She moved as little as possible, said nothing of consequence. She certainly wasn't trying to seem mysterious. Yet he sensed the emotion beneath each carefully chosen word; he saw the pain he'd caused her by saying her name didn't suit her.

She'd been a happy woman once—that much was obvious. Something had happened to turn her into a woman who no longer saw happiness in her life or future.

There was a vivid *life* inside her, yet she lived in dangerous isolation in an arid war zone, in a hut with no amenities, far from family and friends. She was like a sparkling fountain stoppered without reason, a dawn star sucked down into a black hole.

He wanted to know why.

What would she look like if she truly smiled or laughed? To see her hair loose, wearing whatever she had on beneath the soft-swishing burq'a...

The last rays of the setting sun painted the ochre sand a violent scarlet. He blinked—and then it was blocked as her silhouetted form filled the doorway. She took on its hues, softened and irradiated them until she looked ethereal, celestial, a timeless beauty from a thousand Arabian nights, trapped in a labyrinth, needing a prince to save her.

'Do you need more pain relief yet?' A prosaic enough question, but in her voice, gentle and musical, it turned their native language into harps and waterfalls.

Alim blinked again. Stupid, stupid! He'd obviously knocked the part of his brain that created poetry or something. He'd never thought of any woman this way before, and he knew next to nothing about this one. Perhaps that was the fascination: she didn't rush into telling him about herself, didn't try to impress or please him. He was no Aladdin. If she needed a prince, he wasn't one any more, and never would be again. Then he would become a thief: of his brother's rightful position, stolen by a death he'd caused.

And if he kept thinking about it, he'd explode. Time to do what she was doing: make his thoughts as well as their conversation ordinary. 'Yes, please, Hana.'

The shock of sudden pain hit his eyes when she left the doorway and the west-facing door took back the mystical shades of sunset, vicious to his head. It felt like a punishment for turning his saviour into an angel.

He'd obviously been alone too long—but after

three years he still wasn't ready to show any woman his body. If he couldn't even look at himself without revulsion, he couldn't expect anyone else to manage it, let alone find him remotely attractive. Yet there was something about Hana that pulled at him, tugging at his soul—her beautiful eyes, the haunted, hunted look in them…

Hana's unveiled face suddenly filled his vision, and he blinked a third time, feeling blinded, not by the sun, but by her. Catching his breath seemed too hard; speech, impossible.

She didn't seem affected in any way by his closeness. 'Let this swill under your tongue a few moments; it'll work faster that way. You'll feel better soon, and tonight we can sneak in some paracetamol. I'm sorry we have no codeine, it's better for concussion, but stores are limited, as you know.'

Though her words were plain, it felt as if she was doing that thing again, saying too much and not enough. Talking about codeine to hide what she was really feeling.

Had he given himself away, shown that, despite his best attempt at will power, he couldn't stop thinking of her? The internal war raging in him, desire, fascination and self-hate, was so strong it was no wonder she saw it.

Then he realised something. He wasn't itching. He hadn't had the stress-trigger since he'd woken. And the scent of lavender and something else rose gently from his body. She'd rubbed something into his skin while he slept. She'd not only seen the patchwork mess that was his scars, but treated them.

The permanent reminder that he'd killed his brother, his best friend…

Grimly he swallowed the foul brew she handed him, wishing he could ask for something to knock him out again. He handed it back with no attempt to touch her. She didn't want him, and touching her threatened to turn swirling winds of attraction into gale-force winds of unleashed desire that could make him start wanting things he didn't deserve.

'Thanks,' he said briefly, keeping his words and thoughts in prosaic English. Arabic had too many musical cadences, too much poetry for him to hear her speak it, see her lovely form and not be moved to his soul. But she couldn't possibly feel the same after seeing him. He revolted himself, and for more reasons than the physical.

'I'm fine if you need to see to your other patients. I'll sleep now.' He turned from her.

'You should eat first. You don't want to wake up hungry at midnight.'

Irritated beyond measure by her good sense, by her care for what he'd most wanted to hide, he rolled over and snapped, 'If I want food I'll ask for it, *Hana*.' He used cold, deliberate English, to remind her of the danger if she kept distancing herself from him.

In return she made a mocking bow, a liquid movement like the night gathering around her. 'Of course, my lord. I'll bring your food at midnight after caring for you and my patients all day, if such is your wish.' She wasn't smiling, but there was a lurking imp in her eyes…and she still hadn't said his name.

She'd left the hut before he recovered from the surprise that she was making fun of him. Putting him in his place with a few words… He watched her walk away, her body shimmering beneath her shifting burq'a like a fluid dance. 'Hana!' he yelled before he could hold it back.

She turned only her head, but he felt the smile she held inside. 'Yes, my lord?'

Though the term could be a continuation of her

teasing, it made him frown. What did she know about him? 'I'm sorry,' he growled. 'I'll eat whenever you think is best.'

She inclined her head. 'Concussion makes the best of us irritable.' Then she was gone.

It was forgiveness, he supposed, or understanding. He didn't particularly like either—or himself at this moment. He'd lost his inborn arrogance the day Fadi died, or so he'd thought.

Never had he acted with such arrogance with the lowest pit worker, and he'd *never* lost it over a woman's disinterest before. Yet within two hours of meeting Hana he'd become a cliché—a guy in lust with his nurse, cheated because she wasn't entertaining him with flirtation, or distracting him from his pain and lack of control over his body by touching him.

Cheated because she'd touched his body as a nurse, not a woman...by seeing him as a patient—a scarred, angry patient she needed to heal—and not a man.

Growling again, he rolled over and punched the thin pillow, folding it to make it thicker. But rest was impossible while he knew she'd be back.

* * *

It was deep in the night when he came awake with a smothered exclamation—smothered because a hand covered his mouth. 'Not a word,' an urgent voice whispered. The bed dipped and sagged as a soft, rounded backside snuggled into the cradle of his hips. Strange back-and-forth motions made the rusted bed squeak.

The hut was a gentle combination of silvery light and shadow. The tender lavender she wore ignited his senses; the feel of her against his body instantly aroused him. Did she taste as sweet and silky as she smelled and felt on his skin? And her hair was loose, reaching her waist in thick waves, falling over his bare arm in butterfly kisses. Like a paradox, the hand reaching backward, covering his mouth, held him silent in ruthless suppression.

'What are you doing?' It came out as muffled grunts.

'Sweeping my body indents from the ground,' she replied in a fierce whisper. 'I told you to be quiet. Now they'll know we're awake, and will want to know why. Take off your shirt.' She stood, and as he stripped off his shirt her burq'a fluttered to the ground, leaving her only in cami-knickers and a thin cotton vest top. 'Lie on me, and pretend to enjoy it,' she mouthed.

Pretend? The moment he was on her she'd know just how far from a game this was. He thanked Allah that though she'd seen and treated his scars, she couldn't see them in the dark.

Moments later she gasped softly and closed her eyes. Lying stiff and cold beneath him, she managed to whisper, 'Make sounds of pleasure.'

He groaned. Moving against her softness, his body realised how long it had been since he'd loved a woman. It was screaming to him to take this pretence to a perfect conclusion. Yet there'd been an odd note of intensity in her whisper. It went beyond what he would have expected in this situation, and from a widow.

Frowning, he looked down at her, moved by the incandescent beauty of her uncovered face, by the glossy waves of hair shimmering across his pillow and over her shoulders in the moonlight. 'It's all right, Hana, I've done this before.'

'What, you've faked it for killers before? What an adventurous life you've led,' she murmured mockingly in his ear; yet her teeth were gritted, her body so taut with rejection of his touch he thought if he moved at all, he might bounce right off her.

Lifting his face to see her more clearly in the glowing half-light, he saw her eyes were still closed, and there was a sheen of sweat on her brow. She was terrified and trying her best to hide it, but of what was she more frightened: the danger all around them, or the fact that the scarred, ugly stranger lying on her body was obviously ready for action?

Working on the instincts that had saved his life several times, he murmured in a croon he kept for intimate situations, but in English so the men outside wouldn't understand, 'Hana, this goes only as far as it needs to for Sh'ellah's men. You saved my life—you're saving my life again right now. I'd never hurt you or impose my will on you.'

She made a moaning sound that wouldn't fool Sh'ellah's men if they were in the radius of hearing. Her eyes remained squeezed tight shut. 'Thank you.' She arched her body up to his and made a more convincing noise of passion.

Feeling her sweet-scented, fluid body against him, he almost forgot his good resolutions.

Then she stiffened and made a muffled noise, as if finding release. 'Alim,' she cried, using his name for the first time. 'Alim, my love, I've missed you so much!'

Moments later a face appeared at the window; its shadow blocked the moonlight. 'Who is there?' Alim demanded harshly in Maghreb. 'Leave us to our privacy!'

The light reappeared as the head disappeared. He heard a whisper in a mixture of English and another language, but was unable to make it out. He spoke all forms of Arabic, French, German and English, but the African cadences were beyond him.

'Swahili,' she whispered, as tense as her body, though her voice had returned to the voice of a stranger, keeping him at a distance. 'They're saying that Sh'ellah—the local warlord—won't be pleased at this. He had plans for me.'

'I know who Sh'ellah is.' Anyone who'd worked more than a year in the Sahel knew the names of local warlords and what boundaries were where. A wise man also made certain he knew when and where the borders shifted, or he ended up carrion feed. 'He wants you?' he almost groaned in despair. 'That complicates matters.'

'He wants me because I'm young and different to most women in the region. He knows nothing of me. I've always been heavily veiled when his men come. All they or he ever see is my eyes.' She shrugged, in a fatalistic gesture. 'I'm packed and ready to leave. I can go tonight—but you won't make it. We have to wait another day.'

'No.' He knew what she hadn't said: Sh'ellah would think nothing of killing him to have Hana once or twice, before dumping her body in the shifting sands. 'I've worked through injury before. We should get out of here tonight.'

Worried eyes searched his. 'We have to be several kilometres away before they find we're missing, and you were unconscious only hours ago. Fever and concussion aren't conditions to play with.'

Touched by her concern, he whispered, 'I'll be all right.'

She made an impatient gesture. 'No, you won't—but there's no choice. We need to head to the refugee camp. A plane arrives on Wednesdays. It's Thursday now—it will take almost two weeks by foot. With your injuries, we'll need an extra day, travelling by night. We'll take pain-relief tablets with us, a suture kit and extra water.'

'If we head for the truck we don't need to take more than four days. We can drive the rest of the way.'

She frowned. 'That's sixty kilometres away.'

Teeth gritted now, he muttered, 'I'll make it.'

'All right, if you say so.' Those lovely, slanted eyes stared in open doubt. 'I think you can roll off me now. It's customary.'

He wanted so badly to laugh, he did, but made it low and rippling, like a lover's laugh.

He was stunned by her quick thinking and thorough planning. His respect for her grew by the minute. Yet Alim was acutely aware of her near-nude body beneath him, her braless state, the sweetness of her skin and her gentle scent. It was almost a relief to move away, to gain distance— but she snuggled into his arms, making sure the sheet covered the clothes they still wore.

'My love,' she murmured in Maghreb. 'We'll have to take an old suture kit, and bring only the willow-bark infusion,' she whispered, making it seem intimate. 'I'm sorry, but we buried all the new medications. We can't afford to dig them up now.'

'It's okay.' He gathered her against him, kissing her hair—and the lavender filled his head. 'I love your scent.'

Her mouth tightened. She stiffened in his arms, and the budding trust vanished. 'It's not meant to entice. It's to keep off fleas, mosquitoes and bed bugs. Scorpions don't like it, either.'

She sounded frozen. Given the stiff revulsion she'd exhibited only moments before, Alim wanted to kick himself for being so stupid as to think she could want him. Right now, he could think of no reassurance that she'd believe, so he drawled, 'Bed bugs and scorpions…oh, baby, nobody does pillow talk the way you do.'

After a stunned few seconds, she burst out laughing.

Relief washed through him, and he grinned— but the way her face came alive with the smile, the harplike sound of her laughter, made him ache. Now he could see how well her name suited her—or it had once.

Then she whispered, 'I have an aloe and lavender cream for your scars, as well. It looks as though you need pain relief for it. You never finished the plastic surgery you needed, did you?'

She'd ruined their connection by the question, by mentioning his deformity and all its reminders. He moved away from her, trying not to show how hard it was not to fling her away. It was all he could do to ground out a single word. 'No.'

As if she heard his thoughts, she backed off. 'We need to be gone in an hour. There's only one way from the village they won't be covering—

where the wild dogs are. It'll be dangerous, but they usually sleep until dawn. We have to be past their territory by then. There's a small track, an old dried stream we can take, which has some shade for sleeping by day.'

'Right,' he replied, wondering if the feel of his skin against her had done anything but revolt her, having seen him unclothed…having treated his burns as no one had done since he left the private facility in Bern three years ago.

He closed his eyes, squeezing them tight. No wonder she'd been so stiff and cold with him. No wonder she'd turned aside when he'd called her his dawn star. He was a poet from the slag heaps, a monster daring to look upon beauty and hunger for what he couldn't have.

Hana wasn't the kind of woman who'd welcome his touch for his wealth, and he was fiercely glad of that—of course he was. He wasn't that desperate.

'I'll ask one of the men here to pack you a change of clothes. We can only take one each; we need the room for water and medicine. I have dried fruits and energy bars stored in my backpack. We'll fill one canteen with willow-bark infusion for your pain. You'll have to be sparing with it.'

He kept his voice brisk and practical, hiding his turmoil of desire and sickening acceptance of her rejection. 'Travelling at night should help. I have some ibuprofen in my pack I can use. Only a dozen tablets, but—'

She rolled up and sat at the edge of the bed. 'Excellent.' She actually smiled at him. His heart flipped over at the look in her eyes, holding no pity, just approval; and even if she only smiled in relief that he wouldn't be moaning and groaning all the way to the refugee camp, he'd take it. He'd take any piece of happiness she doled out to him, because it felt as if she hoarded it like miser's gold. And it might just mean she wasn't totally revolted by him.

What had happened to her to change her from the happy woman she'd been once, he didn't know—but he had at least a week to find out.

CHAPTER THREE

IT WAS close to three a.m. before they left the hut. Flickering lights a short distance away showed Alim how closely the village was being watched.

'We'll need to commando crawl,' he whispered as they watched another cigarette being lit, another flashlight sweep a slow arc. 'These packs are bulky.'

She nodded. 'And we have to move in silence. They have to believe the villagers know nothing except my husband showed up without warning yesterday, and we disappeared at night.' She handed him a bundle of clothes. 'Put these on. You need to blend into the environment.'

He looked at the clothes, some kind of dun colour, smeared with mud and dirt, and felt intense admiration for her yet again. She thought of everything. 'Can you turn your back?' he asked gruffly, unable to stand that she'd be revolted by his body again.

She nodded and turned away. He felt pity radiating from her, but her practical words made him wonder if the compassion he'd sensed had been the workings of his paranoid imagination. 'You won't be able to wear your clothes until we're out of Sh'ellah's reach.'

As he turned to answer she slipped out of her burq'a with a swift movement, and his breath caught in his throat, remembering her lovely curved body in the knickers and camisole…

He swallowed the ridiculous disappointment. Of course she wore jeans and a long-sleeved shirt with running shoes beneath! What colour he couldn't make out in the murky darkness, but probably brown, like his; her hair looked plaited. She rolled the garment up and stored it in her backpack, and shoved her plait beneath a brown cap.

She shouldered her pack and dropped to the ground, and began belly-crawling. 'Let's go.'

Ignoring the severe pounding inside his head, the light fever that still hadn't abated, he lay down flat and followed her.

It took a gruelling half-hour to make it past the village boundaries to the territory of the wild dogs. Now the moon had set past the village, the delicate filigree beauty around him had faded to a grim, dusty night as thick as the dirt coating them further with every movement.

Alim followed Hana around the hut to the fields, heading towards the only path out, his concentration on two things—being quiet, and trying with all his might not to cough or sneeze. The neckerchief she'd given him to cover his nose and throat was so thickly coated in dirt it was hard to breathe. His scarred skin began to pull and itch in moments.

At the head of the path, she thrust a canteen in his hands. 'Wet the bandanna using as little water as possible, and wring it out,' she whispered in his ear. 'We have to stay flat until we reach the stream bed. Our last opportunity to fill the canteens for fifty kilometres will be there. Move slowly, and try not to let your sweat touch ground. We can't afford to make a sound, or give off any scent. The dogs don't have assault rifles, but they can tear you apart in seconds.'

So that was why she'd only brought dried, wrapped food, and double-wrapped everything in tight-tied bags. Fighting the unwanted arousal her lips against his ear had given him—*damn* his body for all the stupid ideas it had—he nodded and kept following her. Elbows thrust forward and sideways, then a knee, one side then the other, measuring every movement in case it was too big or would dislodge a pebble and make a noise to alert the dogs.

The next hour was excruciating. *Breathing through a wet bandanna, don't move too fast, don't cough or sneeze, don't itch, don't break into a sweat, don't make a noise or you'll become dog meat.* He was forced to follow her, his head pounding with concussion and the stress of aching to go forward, to take the lead and somehow protect her, but this was her turf. She alone knew the way out of danger.

For the first time in his life he had to trust a woman in a life and death situation—but from everything she'd already done, all without flinching or complaint, he knew if there was one woman on earth he could hand control to without fear, it was Hana.

Finally, as he knew he had to breathe clean air or pass out, the flat ground gave way, and they slithered slow and quiet down a little slope; the dust became hard, crusty earth, the cracked mud of a dead stream, and when he heard Hana give a soft sigh he sensed they'd passed at least the first of the current menace facing them.

He slipped the bandanna from his nose and mouth, and dragged in a breath of fresh air without a word. Never had breathing felt so luxurious.

'No water here.' She sighed. 'Our task just got harder, and you're still concussed. Are you sure you're up to this? Once they know we're gone there's no turning back.'

'I can do it,' he reiterated through a clenched jaw. Did she think he couldn't take a little hardship just because of a bump on the head, a touch of fever?

'We have to turn north as soon as we can.' The words breathed in his ear, softer than a whisper, slow and clear, making him shiver in sensuous reaction. 'We still have fifty kilometres to the truck.' The second zephyr of sound stirred his hair and left a small trail of goose bumps.

'Maybe we should leave it where it is and travel south toward the refugee camp by night,' he whispered, as soft as he could. 'If they've found the truck they'll expect us to come for it.'

'You'll never make it to the camp by foot with concussion—it will only worsen without rest. And the boundaries for the warlords change almost daily. If we cross one unseen line, you're dead, and I soon will be, once Sh'ellah finishes with me.'

He shuddered with the force of the flat whisper. 'It'll take three more days to reach the truck, and then we have to backtrack. A hundred and sixty kilometres through enemy lines in a truck so noticeable it practically screams *foreigners*.'

She looked at him, her eyes cool, calm—and how she made him ache with her beauty when she was coated in dust and clumps of mud, wearing a baseball cap and a shirt that looked like charity would reject it, he had no clue. 'Let's go.'

The utter relief to be upright, enjoying the luxury of walking again, flooded him until the headache grew to severe proportions. He said nothing to her until she called for another halt.

After he'd taken some tablets with water, she said, 'We've gone almost as far as we can before sunrise.' She saw him rubbing at his underarm with his arm, trying to scratch unobtrusively. 'How's your skin? Is it itching with all the dirt?'

His jaw tightened and he stopped moving. Yet another reminder: Beauty was letting the Beast know just who he was to her, reminding him what he was to himself. 'I'm fine.'

'I don't want to embarrass you. You won't be

able to travel at night if the grafted skin or the burns rip, bleed or itch. We just crawled more than five kilometres. There has to be damage.'

'I said I'm fine.' He sounded curt with rejection she didn't deserve, but he couldn't help it. 'Give me the cream and I'll do it when I need it.'

Hana sighed. 'There are ways to rub the cream in that optimise stretching and physical comfort for you while we're travelling. It will also give you better sleep. I can see you're uncomfortable with my doing it, but we have four days of hard walking to go, sleeping in dirt and mud that could irritate your skin, and—'

Alim heard his teeth grind before he spoke. 'You're not going to stop arguing until you get your way, are you?'

'Probably not,' she conceded with a gentle laugh.

His head felt like a light and sound show, brilliant stabs of pain shooting from his neck to his eyes. He couldn't manage rubbing the entire length of his scars now if he tried. 'Do it, then.'

The words had been clipped, order from master to servant, but she didn't argue. 'Stay still, and close your eyes.' Her voice was gentle, soothing, stealing into his battleground mind with tender healing.

He felt her undoing the buttons of his shirt... oh, God help him for the male reaction to her touch she'd be bound to see. The sun was beginning to rise.

'Your tension won't help, you know. Breathe deeply, relax and let me make it better.'

She might have been speaking to a child, but her warm, wet hands against his itching, burning scars, filled with beautiful, scented oils, took away any power to speak. He breathed, and felt the irritable tension leaving him, leaving him only aroused.

'That's it, much better. I'm sorry I can't use any water to wash away the dirt, but the olive oil is helping.' Her hands were tender magic, kneading softly, moving in slow, deep circles. Her fingers rotated over his skin, deep then soft; her palms pushed up and around, spreading more oil. 'This solution is fifty per cent cold-pressed olive oil, forty per cent pure aloe juice and ten per cent essential oils of lavender, rosemary and neroli. I make ten litres a month for burns victims or scarring from rifle wounds. A village about forty kilometres from the refugee camp is a Free Trade village, and orders everything I need.'

'Hmm.' She could be reciting the alphabet or

the phone book for all he cared. Her voice was a siren's call, an angel's song; her touch was sweet relief, *bliss*, releasing him from the burning ropes of limited movement, giving him freedom to lift his arm as she moved it to massage where the scar tissue was worst. Though she said and did nothing a nurse wouldn't do for any patient, she made him feel like a man again, because she'd treated him like a man.

'It's feeling better?' she asked softly. She sounded—odd.

'Oh, yeah,' he mumbled. Feeling as if he were floating, he opened his eyes to a slit—and if he weren't so utterly relaxed he'd have started. Hana was looking at his body as she massaged, and it held no revulsion, no clinical detachment. Her eyes in the soft rose light of the sunrise looked deeper, softer…her breathing had quickened…she wet her lips…

Then she looked at his face, her cheeks flushed and her lips parted in innocent, lush surprise, and in her expression was something he'd *never* seen from any nurse.

It was something he'd never seen from any *woman*. Those lovely, slanted almond eyes held something like innocent languor…beautiful, breathtaking, aching *desire*. Good, old-fashioned, honest wanting, woman to man.

Then she saw his eyes open, and the look vanished as if it had never been there. 'Good. I'm glad it helped,' she said, her tone aiming for crisp, but it wobbled a touch. 'Get dressed. If I remember rightly, there's a good overhang a few kilometres away, where we can sleep.'

Was he possibly grinning as widely as he wanted to? 'Why don't we sleep here? You look so tired, and it's been a long, hard day for us both.'

'It isn't far enough from the village.' She was the one now speaking through gritted teeth. 'When we reach the truck, you call the shots. Right now, this is my territory. If you want to live, you're doing things my way.'

Unable to muster up an argument when she'd saved his life again tonight, he shrugged; but he hated that she was right and he couldn't argue, couldn't take charge and protect her somehow. 'Three days,' he said softly. 'Then you'd better believe I'm calling the shots. I'll get you to the refugee camp safely, Hana, that I swear—but you'll obey me, no questions asked.' *And we're going to explore that look you gave me just now,* the man in him vowed, exultant.

She nodded; far from pushing back, there was a suspicious twinkle in her eyes. 'I will obey you joyfully, my lord, for I am a weak woman in need of your strength.' She mock-genuflected before him, touching her forehead to the ground as she spoke. 'It must be the reason why I never left the village before. I was waiting for you to guide and direct me.'

He had to choke down laughter at her unexpected sense of humour. 'Can it, Hana,' he said, using a phrase from one of his former pit crew, 'and let's get going.'

She grinned and bowed again; then, with a grin that held more than a touch of the imp—pretty, so damned *pretty*—she said, 'We should crawl again for a while. It's getting light.'

The prospect made him forget temptation for the present. Alim groaned and dropped to his stomach, but Hana was ahead of him, already wriggling down the hill.

He'd been too busy trying to breathe before to notice how enticing that wriggle was. No—he'd ignored it, thinking it was useless. But after that *look*…

If they'd been anywhere else, had she been another woman…but they were crawling through mud in wild dogs' territory with a warlord's men with assault rifles in every other direction; and this was Hana, who'd frozen beneath him. She deserved his respect, not the burden of unwanted fascination from a man who looked like a damned monster—and he had no magical spell she could reverse with her kiss. The way he looked now was how he'd look for life.

The look had to have been a mistake. He was a nowhere man with no home, no position. He had nothing to offer any woman but ugliness, emotional baggage and a cartload of regrets—and he suspected she had more than enough of her own without taking his on board. Whatever that look had been, she didn't, couldn't want him. He could take that. Just keep commando crawling *and don't look.*

'The creek bed's lined with stones for the next few kilometres. Take these,' she murmured tersely a few minutes later, flipping some leather gloves back at him. 'You'll sweat, but it's better than leaving a blood trail behind for jackals and dogs to find.'

'Thanks,' he muttered back, pulling them on. The skin of his hands had begun to rip, and his clothes were well on their way to becoming shreds, but his hands were the worst. He pulled out a plastic bag from his pack, and shoved it between his T-shirt and the dying jacket to keep his scars from bleeding. If nothing else, it would stop the blood from touching the ground for a few more minutes.

'Come on,' she whispered in clear impatience as she crawled on.

That was the only conversation they had in two hours.

The sun had risen above the eastern rim of the creek wall before she called a halt. 'We're only seven or eight kilometres from the village, but this overhang's the best shelter we'll find for hours. Let's eat and get some sleep.' She leaned against the overhang wall and stretched her back and shoulder muscles with a decadent sigh before rummaging in her backpack.

Refusing to watch—she was killing him with every shimmering movement of her sweetly curved body, her pretty face—Alim sat beside her and stretched too, over and over to work out the kinks—and he was surprised to find the concussion hadn't left him revolted by the thought of food as it always had before when he had concussion, after hitting his head in a race. Despite that his brain was banging against his skull and his eyes ached and burned, his stomach welcomed the thought with rumbling growls.

So he stared when all she handed him was a raisin-nut energy bar.

'Eat it slowly. It's all we can afford to use. I'd only saved enough for me to escape with, so half-rations are all we have.' She surveyed his face, his eyes. 'You're in pain. Take a few sips of the willow bark before you sleep.'

Irritated by her constantly ordering him around, by seeing him as a *patient* after their gruelling trek, he flipped his hand in a dismissive gesture. 'I'll sleep it off.'

'Don't be stubborn. You'll be no use tonight if the pain gets worse. You're less than twenty-four hours from concussion. Take the willow bark, and some ibuprofen with it.'

She was really beginning to annoy him with her imperious, *'don't be stupid'* tone. No woman apart from his mother had ever spoken to him this way. But she was right, so he obeyed the directive, drinking a long swig of the foul medicine with one precious tablet.

'Go ahead and say it.' She sounded amused.

He turned to her, saw the lurking twinkle in

her eyes. There were smile-creases in her face through the caked-on dirt. And no poetry came to his mind. No woman had ever laughed at him, either, unless he'd made a joke. 'What?'

She waved a hand as scratched and cut as his. 'You know, the whole "don't boss me around, I'm the man and in control" routine. You're the big, strong man, and dying to put me in my place. Go on, I can handle it.' Her teeth flashed in a cracked-mud smile.

With her words, his ire withered and died. 'Did it show that much?' he asked ruefully.

She nodded, laughing softly, and he was fascinated anew with the rippling sound. If he closed his eyes, he didn't see the maiden from the bowels of the worst pig-pits, torn and bleeding and coated in mud. She stank; they both did—but he'd rather be here smelling vile beside Hana than in a palace with a princess, because Hana was real, her emotions honest, not hidden because of his station in life. She laughed at him and teased him for his commanding personality, and once the initial annoyance wore off he rather liked it.

'I have no right to assert my authority over you.' Stiff words from a man unused to apologising for anything—but it felt surprisingly good when it was out there.

Flakes of dried mud fell from her forehead as her brows lifted. 'Did that hurt?'

He sighed. 'You really are Australian in your outlook, aren't you? You bow to no man. Your father must have had a really hard time if he was the traditional kind—'

He closed his mouth when he saw the look in her eyes. Devastated. Betrayed. A world of pain unhealed. And hidden deep beneath the pain was defiance. She was fighting against odds he couldn't see, and he sensed she'd refuse to show him if he asked.

If she'd pushed his buttons, she hadn't once pried into his life. He'd done both without even thinking about it. 'Hana…'

She slipped down to lie on the uneven ground. 'I'm going to sleep. I suggest you do, too. We have to go faster tonight.' Her body flipped over as she turned her back on him.

It was another unwanted first in his life—yet it didn't rouse his fierce competitive instincts, but filled him with remorse. She didn't want his apology, because he'd hurt her, a woman who'd

risked her life and given up her home for him, a
man she'd met less than a day ago.

Aching to reach out and touch her, he con-
tented himself by touching her with words...
and this time it wasn't hard. 'Hana, it was a silly
joke, but I hurt you. I'm sorry. I won't pry
again.'

After a moment, she nodded. 'I'm going to
sleep now.' Her voice was thick.

'Goodnight,' he said quietly, feeling an
emotion once totally foreign to him, but now all
too familiar. Shame.

He didn't sleep for a long time, and he suspected she didn't either.

Hana awoke to the heavy warmth of Alim's arm
around her.

It was comforting. It was arousing and it was
beautiful. For the first time in years, she didn't
wake up feeling so utterly alone...

It was a prison trapping her beneath the will
of the man, choking her. Giving in to a man's
wants and desires had subjugated her until she'd
had no life left.

'Get off me.' She fought to make the words
calm. This was Alim, not Mukhtar, whose

criminal acts, blind obsession and selfish needs had ruined her life; but she could feel the rising panic, the memories of the night he'd tried to make his lies come true.

'Hmm?' He moved in closer, holding her. He was aroused, moving against her bottom as though he had the right.

'I said get *off.*' It wasn't a half-request any more. She was almost yelling in her fury and panic to get away.

She felt him stir, this time in wakefulness. 'Huh, what? Oh.' Too slowly, still half asleep, he lifted his arm and moved away. 'Sorry, I wasn't awake,' he mumbled in Gulf Arabic.

Hana struggled for a semblance of serenity, breathing deep, closing her eyes. *I am in control of my life, my decisions. I am—*

I am alone. No man controls me.

There. She'd done it. She opened her eyes and said gently, 'It's all right. I know you didn't mean anything by it.' Her nose wrinkled, and she forced a smile. 'Especially with the way I smell at the moment.' She spoke in English, with a marked Australian accent.

'It's not just you, Sahar Thurayya,' he replied in a strange mixture of English and Arabic. 'I currently offend myself. Alim from the Pigpen.' He chuckled, wrinkling his nose in turn.

Hana had to wrench her gaze from him. His laughter highlighted his scars, taking the handsome face a level higher, to a dark, dangerous male beauty. Combined with his poetic turn of conversation, it was no wonder women fell at his feet. It was a wonder she hadn't already—

Fallen for him. Two days and she was already in way over her head, lost in stormy seas without a life preserver, and he hadn't even touched her. But, oh, she'd touched him and she knew... Did he have any idea how it had felt for her, having her hands on his body? Had she given away the aching throb low in her belly, singing in her blood?

Sahar Thurayya. How many women had he named so exquisitely in the past?

'I think a more appropriate name for me at present would be Dawn Stink,' she said lightly, turning to her backpack. 'Or Evening Stinker, since it's after sunset. Are you hungry, Pigpen, or do you need ibuprofen? We have to eat quickly and go. Sh'ellah's men will be looking for us. I just hope they haven't worked out that you were the truck driver, since we ran.'

'I'd like both food and painkillers, please,' he

said, warm laughter still in his voice. 'So you can call me Pigpen, but never use my name. It's a telling omission,' he added softly—and she knew he'd seen her reaction to his body yesterday, was testing her…

She handed him an energy bar, ibuprofen tablets and a canteen without looking at him. 'I told you before. I'm waiting to see if you live up to it.'

'Well, I certainly live up to Pigpen.' He took the medicine before eating, and she sensed a question coming before he spoke. 'Do you keep all men at a distance, or is it only me?'

The light tone in no way hid the serious intent of the question, but it wasn't aimed at her. The look in his eyes—haunted by bleak self-disgust—told its tale to a trained nurse. She'd seen it many times with burns patients—the horror-filled self-loathing inspired by seeing how they'd look for the rest of their lives. The soul-deep belief that nobody would ever look at them without revulsion, or, worse, they'd always have to endure the awkward, averted eyes and half mumbles of people who didn't know what to say to the poor freak…

What could she say? Nothing, except the truth—that when she'd touched his body, she'd felt he was anything but a freak. That something had awakened in her, beautiful as sunlight on water or the first shooting of a new flower, and now merely looking at him made that budding desire blossom through her veins as fast as grapes on a vine.

She felt herself flushing deeper than the heat of early night allowed. 'Only the ones who put my village at risk and force me to run from my home,' she replied, the quipping note in it a thin sheet covering her pain: both for him and herself. For the first time since leaving Perth, she'd finally felt safe in Shellah-Akbar, as if she belonged somewhere.

Was that why she felt such a kinship to him…because he was a lost soul, just as she was?

A long silence followed; it pulsed with questions he didn't ask. 'I'm sorry, Hana. I came to help but did more damage than good. How unusual for me.'

She turned her face at the self-mocking bitterness, but he'd stood, looking around. For a second time, she opened her mouth and closed it. Despite seeing his near-naked body, sharing a bed with him, faking sex and massaging his body, saving his life and waking in his arms, she didn't know him well enough to attempt comfort.

And yet every time she looked in his eyes, she saw the mirror held up to her face…

When will you learn to love yourself, my Hana? Her mother had first asked that when she was about eleven, and its echoes still rang unanswered in her heart. *Always trying to prove something—that you're the fastest, the smartest, the strongest, most independent, that you don't need anyone—and you never see how vulnerable it makes you.*

Looking at Alim now, she felt the echo of her mother's sadness in the heart of a man she'd only known a short time, a man born to wealth and privilege, raised to rule a nation as the spare, thrust into the position after—

Hana closed her eyes. They *were* two of a kind, seeing themselves through a warped reflection of what they'd done…or should have done. Or what they'd left undone. Nothing was good enough.

She ached to comfort him, but didn't even know how to comfort herself after five years. The only thing he could do to forgive himself was to go back to the world that needed him as much as he needed to be there, to find restoration in his family and his people.

But how could she tell him that when she

couldn't make herself go home, couldn't face her own family?

'How bad will it be for the village?' he asked as he turned to look at the north.

She glanced at him, saw the readiness to blame himself for anything that happened at Shellah-Akbar, and deliberately softened her tone. 'They'll tear it apart to find the supplies—but they've done that before, and found nothing.' She chewed her energy bar, choosing to hide the worst from him, and acknowledging that she felt some need to protect him. He was carrying enough guilt on those broad shoulders. 'I told Malika and Haytham to hold to the story that you're my husband, and we ran because we overheard the men speaking about Sh'ellah's plans for me.'

'Will they believe it?'

If they told Sh'ellah that, he'd go on a rampage to find me and kill you. She kept her tone gentle. 'They might believe it. If they can't find the food, they'll have nothing else to go on.'

'Where do you hide the food?' he asked, his voice thick, and she knew she hadn't fooled him a bit.

She carefully didn't look at him as she said, 'We trade on the old custom of fear of the dead, and bury everything in graves, usually beneath the coffins of the children.'

'Your people will do that?' he asked, sounding startled.

Understanding what he was asking, relieved to take the topic from anything that hurt him so deeply, she nodded. 'At first they resisted, so I did it myself. Then, when Sh'ellah's men wouldn't disturb the dead, and the spirits didn't destroy me for what I'd done, they helped me. I've found many people will put aside the most frightening of their customs and beliefs in their need to survive,' she said quietly, 'to save their children.' Her parents would have done the same. It was always family first...which was why they'd had to choose: marry Hana off quickly to a bad man, or ruin Fatima's chances of ever finding a good man. Fatima had only been seventeen.

It was said that to understand was to forgive... but though she'd always understood the dilemma her parents had faced, choosing to bow to community pressure, and sacrifice one sister for the sake of the other, she'd never found forgiveness in her heart. *I was innocent, too! Did you ever for a moment think I hadn't done what he said?*

Alim turned towards the south, squinting in concentration. 'What will you do now?'

'Go to the refugee camp.' But she couldn't stay there for long; it was too public, too exposed. Her father might have sent someone to look for her there, ask for her by name, or for a woman with her description, including the Australian accent—which was why the burq'a came everywhere with her, and she spoke Maghreb whenever possible. 'Then they'll reassign me to another village that needs a nurse.'

'There's a dust cloud about four kilometres away, heading towards us,' he said, frowning to the south.

'Pick up anything that tells them we were here, use your jacket to cover footprints and body imprints and let's go,' she said tensely. She pulled a ripped cotton sheet from her backpack in four pieces, and tied two to his ankles, and to hers. 'It's far from perfect, but the ground is so dry our footprints will be difficult for their trackers anyway.'

'Do we run, or try to jump from rock to rock as long as we can?'

Caught by the innate wisdom—he'd assumed they'd keep hiding in the creek bed, and he was right—she smiled at him, and found her foolish lungs trapping air inside her when he smiled back. 'Tonight you've earned your name, Alim. The rocks, as fast as safety allows.'

'I have my moments—as do you, happy woman.' He winked at her. She could tell he was pleased—her foolish heart certainly leaped at the smile, at the unexpected emotional intimacy—and the inexplicable sense of oneness she'd felt with him from the first moment she'd seen him torn and bleeding in the truck came back in double force. She couldn't tear her gaze from him—and the worst part was it was as emotional as it was physical. She felt *bound* to him somehow.

'We have to go,' he said softly, his eyes warm, dark as he smiled, and his mouth—*oh…*

'Yes,' she whispered, her eyes locked on his half-smile, lips parted, breathing fast. A thrill so strong it almost hurt ran through her, breasts to fingertips. Her body swayed towards him.

He bent until his breath whispered along her lips like a tender kiss. 'We must go now, Sahar Thurayya. I won't let him take you, not while there's breath in my body. Let me go first this time, my star. I'm actually useful at jumping rocks and finding the most stable ones.'

She couldn't speak, aching for the almost-touch…but she managed a nod.

He bent to pick up the packet from his energy bar and made a mess of the soil where they'd slept, and the moment passed—no, it didn't pass; it slipped into his pocket, into her heart, awaiting its chance. And she knew it would come.

She followed him from rock to rock, leaping like mountain goats, her mind in turmoil, her heart and body fighting for—what? There could be nothing between them. She'd only known him two days, yet she ached and hurt with desire for him as she never had for any man.

Taking the lead yet asking her first was just another way he'd shown her the man he was. Alim was a complex blend of traditional and modern, Arabic and man of the world—but even with his humour and his kindness, and a smile that melted her inside, he was still a man; and she wasn't free to feel attracted to him, or to dream of a future.

She was trapped…if not by this life on the run, then by tradition, her father's pride—and by Mukhtar. She might not have made the vows herself, but her father had done so for her, and he'd signed the marriage certificate in her name.

She hated the man her father had given her to in marriage, but she had no choice. Mukhtar had made sure of that.

CHAPTER FOUR

THEY'D been leaping and running alternately for a couple of hours when Alim's brain began crash-banging against his skull and his feet no longer felt certain on the ground.

He came to an abrupt halt. Hana would have barrelled into him if she hadn't had superb self-control—or if she hadn't been watching him for signs of collapse. She stopped right behind him and said, softly, 'Ibuprofen and water?'

Yes, she'd been watching, waiting for him to fall. She was thoughtful and high-principled, imperious queen and caring Florence Nightingale rolled into one. She might be the daughter of a miner, but a woman with Hana's integrity and inner strength was destined for some high place.

His mouth and throat, even his lungs felt scorched, parched as the earth beneath their feet.

'Yes.' It took all *his* control not to groan aloud. 'Please,' he ground out.

In moments she'd handed them to him, and he drank gratefully.

'Drink it all, Alim. You're dehydrated. We still have four canteens left, and we'll hopefully reach a small well by nightfall tomorrow.'

She knew her way through this arid wasteland. She'd worked out her escape route well in advance. It told him far more than she intended...and she'd called him by name again. Even if it was because she currently felt superior to him, he felt a grin form. From the moment she'd touched him, her guard had been falling. As unbelievable as it was, she did desire him.

He left a few mouthfuls of water for her. 'You need to drink too, or you'll end up with a dehydration headache, and then where will we be?' he teased, even through the pain.

She mock-bowed again, bending right over and peering up at him from about the level of his hip. 'Yes, O my master,' she rasped, and he chuckled as she took the canteen. She'd had the cringing tone of Gollum down pat. 'Please take this and rub it on your forehead—it will help until the tablets take effect.' She held out a small dark bottle to him.

He took the tiny dropper bottle from her, and sniffed its contents. 'Peppermint and lavender oils?'

She grinned. 'Yes, it is, and no, we are *not* going to use it to kill the stink of sweat and mud. We need it for headaches when we run out of ibuprofen. So use it sparingly, here—' she pointed to his forehead '—and here.' She touched his pulse-point in his throat, a brief, sweet flutter of a muddy finger, too soon over.

She waited until he'd rubbed some of the fragrant oils on his forehead before lifting the canteen to her lips, drinking so fast he knew she'd been as thirsty as he.

She must be closer to dehydration than him. She'd been giving him more water all along, citing his concussion as the reason.

'You love caring for people,' he remarked as she packed away the oil bottle and the empty canteen. 'And being in control,' he added, teasing her to lessen her suspicions that he was digging again—which he was.

'Yes, I guess I do.' She flashed him a rueful smile, her white teeth startling in the darkness and her dirty face. 'It's why I became a nurse—that, and my father wouldn't have allowed me

any other profession without being married first.'
A shadow crossed her face, her smile vanished.
She said no more.

'It must be killing you, not seeing your family,'
he said, taking a stab in the dark. Until now he'd
thought her alone in the world. Now he sensed
the truth lay deeper.

Her eyes sparked in the night with dangerous
fire. 'Is it killing you?'

He stared at her unblinking for a moment, and
decided to meet the challenge. 'You know who
I am, why I'm in Africa.' *Because it's as far from
my privileged, fast-lane life as I could find on
short notice...where they wouldn't think to look
for the missing sheikh.*

And he'd stayed because—well, because he
had to. For the first time in his life, he wasn't the
second heir, Fadi's replacement, or The Racing
Sheikh. The people here, from the aid agencies
to the villagers, needed his skills, not for enter-
tainment, but to save their lives.

Hana bowed again, but without the impish fun,
the softness in her eyes vanished. 'It wasn't hard,
my lord. Your face is famous. Your disappearance
became a worldwide interest story.'

'Especially among our people,' he agreed

through gritted teeth. She knew too much about him and his secrets, and he had to piece hers together by all she didn't say.

Even in the black of night, he saw her face pale. 'Stop there.'

'So you are from Abbas al-Din? Are you on the run from your father, or the husband you claim you don't have?' he pressed, wanting something, any part of her, the vulnerability and loneliness he felt beneath layers as strong and as fragile as the burq'a she'd worn the first day.

'Stop.'

She wasn't looking at him, but her tension was so palpable she looked like a string pulled as far as it would go without snapping. 'All right.' After a few moments he asked, 'Did you know who I was from the start? Was that why you saved me?'

She sighed. 'Not in the truck, or when I stitched you—but I knew by the time Sh'ellah's men arrived. Be grateful for that—if I hadn't known I wouldn't have hidden your face, and they'd have taken you. As for coming with you now, I had no choice—but I would have saved anyone who needed my help.'

He could feel the truth in every word. He

should be grateful that she'd been honest with him, but it hurt far more than it should have.

Two days was all that had passed since they'd first met, yet she meant more to him than she should. Possibly because she'd saved him so many times; possibly because she was one of his own, and he hadn't been aware how deep his hunger ran to be with his own people again—

And most probably because she was Hana, his dawn star who shone in a dark world: an honest woman who refused to lie even when it could save her.

'So you're saying I'm just anyone? One of hundreds you've probably saved?' His voice was rough with the weird mix of anger and gratitude simmering in him.

She turned her face to him, frowning. Flecks of dirt fell from her cheeks with the movement. 'Would you *rather* I saved you because of who you are?'

'No,' he muttered. She was right; he wouldn't want that. So what *did* he want from her?

That was the trouble; his emotions felt as confused as his concussed brain. But from the start, Hana had humbled him, amazed him, fascinated him—and the combination was deadly for a man who had as many secrets as he did. But she'd known who he was all along, and said nothing until he'd asked, until he'd prodded her pain and she'd responded without thought.

She'd treated him like any other man. She'd laughed at him, ordered him around—desired him with honest heat...

Or had she? Had everything she'd said and done been a lie, centred on fascinating the deformed, lonely sheikh until he was her emotional slave?

'So what's your plan when we return to the world?' he drawled to hide his sudden, blinding fury. 'There's probably quite a reward for my safe return to Abbas al-Din. Or are you hoping for an even better reward than money—my mistress, perhaps? Or even my wife, if you think wealth and position can make up for having to tolerate me in your bed?'

He didn't know what he expected her to do—slap him, toss half the energy bars and water at him and demand they go their separate ways...cry and protest her innocence...furiously remind him she'd saved his life before she'd known his identity—

Shame scorched him as he remembered that. He opened his mouth—

But then she finally responded: wild, almost jackal-like laughter. 'You have got to be kidding me,' she gasped, her face alight with hard mirth. She doubled over, her gusts of laughter growing stronger by the moment. 'I'm seducing you!'

Alim stared at her, shocked into silence. 'What's so funny?' he asked at last, when she seemed to be sliding into full-on hysteria.

She straightened, still chuckling, but the eyes that met his were diamond-hard, glittering with an emotion he couldn't stand to see in her. 'Until you resume your true identity and position in Abbas al-Din, my lord, you have no right to demand answers of me. Until then, I can safely promise I will *not* be calling the media to collect any reward, and I certainly won't be seducing you at any time in the near future. So *ironic…*' She shook her head and slid down to the ground, laughing with that cold cynicism he'd never thought to see in his deep-principled, caring saviour.

The irony was lost on him, but he saw one thing clearly: something had made Hana run from her world, and he'd tapped into it with his anger—and his believing the worst of her after she'd saved him so many times. That was what it came down to.

What had he *done*?

Through a painful stone lodged in his chest, he forced out, 'Hana, I—'

'Don't waste time with an apology you won't mean and I won't believe.'

Her cool words broke into the apology budding in his heart, stopping it dead. She was back on her feet, shouldering her backpack. 'Silence would be best at this point. Let's go.'

Her face was remote, cool as ice water splashed in his face—and again, she'd treated him like she would any man who deserved her withdrawal. Despite recognising him, he wasn't a figurehead to her. He was Alim, and she was showing him the consequences of his unleashing his foolish mouth on her.

Since meeting her he'd butted in on her private world, hurt her and forced her to flee her village, destroying her fragile illusion of safety in Shellah-Akbar. And now he'd added humiliation to the list, treating her as a mercenary predator willing to sleep with him for what she'd get from it.

The worst of it was he had a feeling that, no matter how ashamed he felt, Hana was shouldering a far greater burden from his unthinking accusations.

* * *

It was almost sunrise again. They'd been walking ten hours, and Hana had felt Alim's remorse walking between them like a shadow-creature the whole time. She'd felt it hovering there, aching for release, for the past twenty-four hours.

She'd felt his shame through the last of their night-walk last night, his anxiety to make it better through his care that she rest her head on his jacket as she slept today. She'd heard his worry in his insistence she drink first, and the bigger share of the energy bar he'd given her, saying with an uneven laugh that it held no appeal after the fourth or fifth bar. But though he didn't push her or talk about it, she knew what he craved.

Forgiveness. A simple word, but so hard to practise when people she cared for, people she trusted believed the worst of her, over and over; and now, with a weary acceptance, she knew Alim had been added to that list. People she'd trusted who'd betrayed her. *People that she cared for, who believed she was…*

Oh, God help her, she cared for him, and that he'd been able to accuse her of those things at all meant he'd believed it. Whether he'd believed for a moment or an hour or a lifetime didn't matter; whether it was based on his lack of self-belief didn't change it. It was done, he'd said it, and her heart felt like a lump of ice in her chest. The only way she could survive the next few days and save him, and herself, was to close down until she said goodbye to him for ever.

She couldn't go through it again, couldn't care, couldn't *trust* and have it betrayed, leaving her— like *this*. All she could do was slam the shutters down on her heart, show nothing and hope to heaven she could survive this bleak emptiness a second time.

As they prepared for breakfast the silence seemed so loud it screamed over the sounds of the creatures waking for the day in the scrubby hills to the west. The hope and the need for her forgiveness crouching beneath his compliant quiet filled her stomach with sick churning until she couldn't swallow a single mouthful of her food.

She couldn't give him the absolution he wished for—but she had to say something, so she blurted the first thing that came to mind. 'You haven't used the oil on your skin for a while. It must be itching.' She rummaged in the backpack, and thrust the oil for his scars at him.

After a moment, he took the bottle. 'Thank you. It is uncomfortable.' With an unreadable look he stripped off his shirt, and slapped some of the oil onto his skin, rubbing briefly and moving to the next spot, slap and rub, as if he were taking a shower.

Typical male! With an impatient sigh, she snapped, 'Stop that, it won't do a thing to help.' She rubbed her hands together for warm friction, and took over. Spreading her fingers wide, she moved her hands over his skin, slow and deep, and gritted her teeth against the pressure building in her throat, the moan of pleasure at touching him bursting to be free. 'This is how you do it,' she said as coldly as she could manage, to hide her reaction. 'You have to let the oils penetrate the muscle as well as skin, and soften the scar tissue or it won't stretch.'

'Ah...I—I see.' The words were a low growl, a masculine equivalent of purring desire whispering in her head, symphony to harmony. Was it because her hands were on his body again, or the physical release from the pulling pain the oils gave? 'I think this skill took a long time to learn,' he grated out.

'It, um, did take a while.' Striving to master the craving, she gulped again. Fighting hot-honey temptation...but there were no scars on his neck, or up into his hair. She had no excuse to touch there…and the anger and betrayal that had held her captive for over a day was flying faster than a skier on a downhill run. 'I took a course on massage therapy for burns patients after I worked—at a burns unit,' she said, remembering in time not to give away more information than necessary. 'When I graduated, that's what I wanted to do, work in a burns unit.'

'You don't find the sight of the mangled flesh—repulsive?'

That crazy skier had just flown straight off a cliff, and the ice surrounding her heart cracked, letting out steam. 'I hate the endless agony of burns. I wish there were some new way invented to heal the scars, stop the pulling of the flesh, limiting movement. I *hate* that almost everyone who has suffered extensive burns no longer feels human.' She continued the movements of her hands over his skin, slow and steady, deep and soothing…healing his body as she looked in his eyes. She saw the seething mass of self-revulsion inside, and her heart lurched and sloughed that ice right off, leaving only honesty. 'But, no, I don't find anything about you repulsive—except the ugliness that comes from your mouth.'

The shimmer of his eyes, before they closed, told her how much he felt as he said, 'You have no idea how I regret what I said.'

'What hurt most was that you meant it,' she said quietly—and she was amazed how good it felt to say it, to say to him what she hadn't been able to say to her father.

'Only because of this,' he replied, his hands moving to hers, stilling them, and she caught her breath at the intimacy, at the look in his eyes, so stark and unashamedly vulnerable. 'It isn't you, Hana. If I could take the words back—'

She shook her head, shivering in a breath. 'But you can't, and I can't forget.' She moved her hands until he took his away. 'I can't give you the absolution you want.'

'But you give me what I need—and right now, what I deserve,' he said softly, lifting one oil-soaked hand in his, and kissing her palm—not in sexual intent, but in reverence, and tears rushed into her eyes as her foolish heart leaped of its own accord, whispering the words her mind refused to accept. 'You're honest with me, Hana. You don't defer to me, to what I am.'

She pulled her hand away, and lifted her chin. 'What you were. You're what I am now, a runaway helping others to try to forget what we left behind.'

'No matter what position we hold in life when we're born, we all spend our lives trying to prove we're worth something, or better than others believe we are.'

The dark heart of all she'd tried to achieve since she'd fled to Africa lay before her, exposed and bleeding. She couldn't answer but turned from him, wrapping her arms around herself in a pitiful attempt at comfort. Her wet, oily hands soaked into her shirt, and the restful lavender drifted up. She wondered why it made her feel so sad.

'Sweet Hana.' The soft murmur came close to her, and she shivered in uncontrollable yearning. 'Strong Hana, who's always giving to others, always saving them…but who comes to Hana when she needs a saviour? When was the last time anyone held you, or saw how alone you are in your strength?'

She couldn't breathe. The jagged lump of tears filling her throat stung her eyes.

'Muddy angel,' he whispered, so close his warmth touched inside her shuddering soul.

'You're more beautiful in your honesty than any woman I've seen in diamonds and silk.'

Tears splashed down her cheeks. 'Stop. I want to hate you.'

Closer, inch by inch, until his arms covered hers, crossing over from behind, and at last she felt strong, no longer alone, if only for a moment. 'But you can't, can you?'

Slowly, she shook her head—and that hurt most of all, that she couldn't hate him. 'I—I don't know you well enough to hate you.'

'Was it Omar Khayyam who wrote that when souls entwine, they're never strangers, though they know each other only moments—and when souls repel, they'll never know each other in a lifetime?' he whispered behind her ear.

She dragged in a breath. 'I don't know the poets. I'm only a miner's daughter.'

'You're a queen in a nurse's skin.' He drew her stiff form back, caressing only her hand, until her body relaxed. 'You're my Sahar Thurayya, my brave, beautiful dawn star. I'm so glad you can't hate me—but can you forgive me for my self-absorbed stupidity?'

Millimetre by millimetre, she moved until she

leaned into his warm strength, rested her head against his shoulder.

'Give me one final chance, Sahar Thurayya— a chance for you to trust me again. I want that one chance more than I've ever wanted anything.'

She turned to look up at him in wonder. How did he know? How could he guess the words she'd heard in her head a thousand times, with her father's voice? Could he know what *healing* it brought her, hearing them while she rested in his arms?

'I want a second chance with you more than anything but one thing. You know what that is,' he added, low, and the endless anguish made the mirror of their self-hate melt like a final barrier. He was speaking of his grief, of his brother.

'Yes, I know.' Her voice cracked. She couldn't give him stumbling words that wouldn't comfort, or platitudes that wouldn't help. Only he could come to terms with Fadi's death and find peace...but there was one thing she could give him, and she found it wasn't as hard as she'd thought it would be. Her forehead rested on his shoulder. 'Alim...'

The darkness in his voice lifted like the sun rising behind them. 'Thank you.'

Neither moved to leave each other's arms.

After a long time, Hana twisted in his arms to touch the scarred flesh on his shoulder and chest. 'Some time you're going to need more surgery,' she murmured, not massaging but caressing him. Strangers' souls entwining with the touch. *Trust.*

'Yes,' was all he said in reply, his hand lifting to cover hers, and he smiled. *Healing.*

Hana woke with a start in a shallowed-out rut in the creek bed. Once more she felt the heat and weight of Alim's arm around her waist; but the warmth of his body against hers, and the sweat running down her skin from the late afternoon heat and his closeness, wasn't what disturbed her the most. Something was wrong.

Then she heard the voices, two men speaking in Swahili coming closer—

By the tension in Alim's body, she knew he was awake. Slowly, he parallel-lifted his legs, keeping them tense and straight. He pushed her legs up with the movement of his, until their legs rested at a ninety-degree angle to his hips. It was intimate, shocking in its sensuality, and necessary to keep them alive. Their bodies were out of the revealing sunlight, backpacks pushed against the curve of her belly.

He rolled them both until she sat on his bunched-up knees. 'Get up and flatten your body against the wall,' he whispered in her ear as he rubbed his back against the damp sides of the creek bed. 'Get in as far as possible, take the backpacks with you and don't breathe out loud.'

She nodded, and, looking down at the ground first for any rocks that could move under her feet and give them away, she moved with agonising slowness until she stood beneath the small overhang of the creek wall, holding the back-packs in shaking hands. She pushed into it until she moulded the mud, turning her face so she could breathe.

The top of her head was against the overhang. Alim was too tall to hide.

Anxiety for him overwhelmed her. She rolled her head to the other side, until she could see him—and wanted to laugh. He lay flat against the thick mud, in the worst patch of mud, stinking with rotting plants and animal droppings, his face turned into the wall. His rolling had turned his hair, and the few remaining clean patches of his clothes, the hue between sand and mud.

He was nothing but a few lumps of mud—as was she.

The warlord's men moved like snails along the creek. Her heart pounded so hard she wondered that the men seeking them couldn't hear her uneven breaths. The men talked almost right above them; one flicked a still-smoking cigarette into the creek bed behind them. Hana, who could never stand the smell, had to fight against choking or coughing. But finally the men moved off, searching further down.

Alim nudged her with his foot, pushing her closer in, and she knew what he wanted. *Stay still a bit longer.* Back aching with the unaccustomed inward curvature of her spine, breathing in more mud and nicotine smoke than air, she held to the wall a few more minutes.

They waited until the sound of an engine gunning up and roaring off told them they were alone. 'I thought I'd choke if I had to breathe in any more of that.' Alim rolled over and flicked the cigarette away, then drew in a deep breath. 'Ah, the delight of fresh—well, muddy-fresh air.' He grinned, his teeth a bright dazzle between the ruthless sunshine and the mud coating him.

She wanted to giggle at his comical appearance, but the fear still walked too close; she was close to shivering in forty-degree heat. 'We can't afford to wash until we reach that waterhole, but would you like to smear some lavender and peppermint oil on, to ease the stink?'

He smiled. 'I think I was lying in warthog droppings, so, yes, I'd love that, thanks.'

Hana stared at him. His smile—it was different. Something inside it—the look in his eyes—made her catch her breath, almost forgetting their recent danger.

She'd *never* forgotten the danger she'd been in since arriving in Africa. But though the threat was more real now than at any other time, her pounding heart was not in fear, but in the strangest, pulsing excitement…

She could barely look at him as she handed him the bottle; but when, in handing the bottle back for her turn, his fingers brushed hers, she wanted to see his face, to know if he meant that look, that slow-burning desire. If he—

'We should move on,' she said when she was done. She cursed the breathlessness in her tone—it must give away the aching in her eyes. What was it about this man that turned her into this aching mass of *need*, living for the next time he looked at her, touched her? Was it because he was out of reach? Or that he was right here within her reach?

After a moment, he shook his head. 'No, this isn't the time.' The laughter had vanished from his eyes; they'd turned dark, sombre. 'We should wait here until dark.' As he'd done from the hour they met, he was reading more into her simplest words than she wanted him to.

Seeing inside her soul…

'Whatever you say, boss,' she quipped, handing him a canteen of semi-clean water. 'What I wouldn't give for a camera now.'

He frowned, asking without words.

She pointed at him, grinning with the teasing that was her best cover against self-betrayal. 'This is how the sheikh of Abbas al-Din hides from the world: he seeks oil in new and foreign territories in his own special way.'

He broke out into soft laughter.

Hana stared at him, riveted by the mud-encrusted, strong, beautiful face. Despite it being her joke, she couldn't share his laughter; she could only watch in strange, burning hunger. He laughed as if he meant it. He laughed as if he hadn't truly laughed in a very long time.

She couldn't drag her gaze away even when he looked up and the laughing words he'd been about to utter dried on his tongue. He looked at her and she wasn't fast enough, couldn't hide what she was feeling. His eyes widened for a moment, then turned soft with languorous intent. 'Hana, don't look at me like that unless you mean it.'

She couldn't answer, couldn't turn away, just kept looking at him, aching, wishing, hoping. She forgot all the reasons why she could never give herself to any man, let alone this one. All she saw was that look in his eyes…

Ah, he was on his feet…one step, two—and his hand lifted, reaching out to her. Asking, not demanding—but, oh, the look in his night-pool eyes compelled her. Of its own volition her arm lifted, her hand rested in his.

A smile curved his fine, sensitive mouth, those fathomless eyes. 'Lovely Hana, always giving to others,' he murmured, his fingers moving over hers, and she was lost. 'You brought me from death and darkness, gave me a second chance at life. Isn't it time you learned to live?'

His thumb slipped between their linked palms, and caressed.

Her eyes fluttered closed as her body wandered the maze of the rush, the overwhelming rush of her blood, the soft singing of feminine desire swelling to a chorus in her. 'Alim...' She couldn't breathe. The lightest touch and he'd wrapped her inside the sweetest, most heady chains she'd ever know.

'I love the way you say my name, as if you mean it,' he whispered.

'Ah,' she whispered back, unable to say more. Her hand moved in his, asking, pleading. *Just keep touching me.*

His thumb brushed her palm, a hardly-there touch that sent her hurtling into a magnificent *aliveness* she'd thought she'd never feel, or understand: the exquisite beauty between man and woman. There was nothing but here and now, and Alim...

A butterfly caress over her lower lip, the single touch of his finger, and her knees trembled. She gasped in a shaking breath. She buried her face in his chest. 'Alim, please...'

'What do you want?' he murmured into her hair. 'Ask me, just ask me, and it's yours.' His body brushed hers and she made an incoherent little cry of need.

'I—I don't—more,' she whispered, her body moving in time to his. 'Oh, please, more.'

Ah, those strong arms were around her, those fine-fingered hands on her back, bringing him close to her, so close his body warmth filled her soul, his light chased away the years she'd spent hiding in darkness. 'I was wrong. Your name does suit you,' he murmured.

The scent of mud and his man's heat and the oils he wore intoxicated her. Her breathing turned erratic again as she raised heavy-lidded eyes to his. 'Why?' she whispered, not because he waited for her answer, but because he waited for her. From somewhere deep inside the pounding, the delicious throbbing controlled her.

Could he see it? Did he know how *much* he affected her?

His voice was tender and rough. 'You bring happiness wherever you go. You have pockets filled with sunshine you hand to others even when your life's at risk. You've brought me to life, filled my soul with laughter…and passion.' A current of hunger as hot as the wind blowing above them moved from him to her, and back.

'I have?' Uncertain of all these new feelings in her body, she wet her mouth with her tongue, and saw his eyes turn dark and light at once. A tender, knowing smile curved his lips.

She wanted to touch the smile with her fingers…to touch him, just touch him.

'You do. You're good for me, Sahar Thurayya.' Slow, gentle, his hand reached to her face, curving around her cheek. A tiny moan escaped her lips. His thumb caressed her mouth. Her eyes closed and she drank it in, thirsting and starving for this man, a stranger just days before, a man as far above her reach as the most distant star. But none of that mattered when he could make her feel like a priceless treasure, like a woman wanting a man…

Her head rolled back, taking in the caress as it moved along her jaw to her ear. 'Why am I good for you?' Her voice was breathless, barely above a whisper. *More, please keep touching me.* She moved against him again, delicious, sweet pain and exquisite hunger.

His hands cupped her throat, and she felt another tiny purr leave her lips, felt her body sway with desire. 'You know why, my dawn star.'

'Say it,' she whispered, her fingers trailing over his hand, his arm. Flaking mud fell unnoticed as she found patches of skin, warm, rough, male.

'You make me laugh at myself,' he murmured. 'You give me a new perspective. You've opened my eyes to the world, to problems far greater than my own. I thought I was alone in this desire, but you want me, too. You want me so much you can't even hide it. But you know that.' Butterfly-soft fingers trailed down her throat.

Yes, yes, I know. And he now knew how much she desired him. She'd given herself away, had let him inside her, to see a small piece of her heart and secrets. How long would it be before he knew everything…?

As far as she was concerned, Mukhtar's rights to her were nil. Her father had severed the engagement to Latif as if it didn't matter—and Latif had walked away so fast she'd wondered if she had a disease. Nobody believed her. *Nobody.*

And with that thought, the moment was gone. Just thinking of Mukhtar, and the flame inside her began burning bright with pain and betrayal.

'Hana?' The look in his eyes hurt her.

Gulping down a huge wave of disappointment, she dropped her chin and moved out of his touch. 'That was rather irresponsible of us.' She tried to inject lightness into her tone.

His hand remained in the air, reaching out to her for a moment, before it fell. 'Yes, it was, given where we are and the danger we're in.' His eyes searched her face…seeking out her secrets as if she'd given him the right.

'We need to go back to sleep.' She heard the choked note in her voice, and cursed it. But desire was too new to her to fight; she didn't have the weapons.

'You sleep, Hana. One of us needs to keep watch in case they come back. Don't argue with me,' he added, his voice hard, when her mouth opened. 'The concussion's barely there now. You don't need to watch over me any more.'

She frowned, her eyes searching his face for fatigue or stress.

He turned away. 'Just do it, Hana.' He added with a sigh when she shook her head, 'After a man becomes this aroused, it's difficult to roll over and sleep. If you stay awake, I'll take it as a signal that you want me to keep touching you…and you want to keep touching me.'

The blunt words shocked her, fascinated her. She'd aroused him with such a simple touch of her fingers over his hand and arm, a few brushes of her body against his?

*I was aroused only by the way he looked at me.
I was totally lost in him.*

She still was aroused…and an hour later, lying
rigidly still, she wondered if it was the same for
women as men, because she couldn't stop the
heated pounding deep inside, the lilt and throb
of her blood, when the cause of her sweet burden
sat but three feet away in exactly the same pre-
dicament as her own, guarding her rest.

CHAPTER FIVE

FUNNY, but of all the attacks Alim had imagined during their crawling and jumping life on the run, the one he hadn't thought of was the most likely to kill them. He'd thought of lions, rhinos or hippos, even a warthog, but not—

He awoke with a start. He'd finally fallen asleep after hours of watching her. He'd known the whole time that she wasn't asleep; she was restless with the same ache of desire low in her belly that he felt, and knowing that only made it worse.

How could she have seen the mess of congealed flesh and the patches of grafted skin covering his torso, and still want him, be so vividly aroused by his touch? In all his life he'd never known a woman to have such an extreme reaction to anything he did, even his smile. He'd laughed, and she couldn't drag her eyes from him…

And when he'd talked of Fadi, instead of the

usual numbness and agony combined, the feeling
of being stuck in an unending dark tunnel, he'd
felt—relief. Not forgiveness—he doubted that
would ever come—but...he'd thought of Fadi
that night, and smiled, remembering other parts
of that day. The way big brother had done his
best to keep up with him around the track; the
laughing challenges; the *relaxed* grin on Fadi's
face. Alim hadn't seen him let go of his responsibilities since—since he'd had to take over
running the small nation at the age of twenty.

He'd forgotten the joy of that day, until Hana
reminded him without even asking.

Could the woman who was his saviour also
become his miracle? Was it possible?

At last she'd slept as dusk began filling the sky
with its violent magenta. Though he'd known it
was time to leave, sleep had rushed on him
without his knowledge.

How long had he slept? Day had long since
given way to the deep velvet of night—

Rustling in Hana's backpack alerted him to
why he'd awoken so suddenly. Some small
creature had found their stores.

He grabbed the bag and tipped it upside
down—and swore when he saw the damage

wrought by the two small mouse-like creatures trying to bolt with their booty. The plastic double bags that were supposed to stop any scent escaping were torn to shreds, and the mice had already eaten two bars, by his count, and were into another two. With an incoherent sound of frustration, he dived for one of the bars the creatures were running off with in their mouths.

The noise alerted Hana. 'What is it?'

'Mice,' he muttered, jumping after the scurrying mouse, and yelling in triumph as he managed to snatch the bar back—or what remained of it.

With a cry of distress, Hana dived after the other creature with one of the bars, but it disappeared down a hole in the creek bed with its find.

Hana closed her eyes in despair. 'We couldn't afford to lose a single bite of food. We're only travelling eight to ten kilometres a night as it is. Without enough food, we'll never make it to the refugee camp.'

'We'll make it,' he said, touching her face in reassurance.

She jerked away so hard he thought she'd fall. 'Do you think royal commands will magically protect us from starvation, my lord?' She rubbed her eyes in tired frustration. 'Have you ever *had* to worry that you'll starve to death?'

He couldn't answer. Even on the run, he was a multibillionaire who helped others by choice, but could and did return after a food and medicine run to his luxury villa on the beach at Mombasa. If he was far from home he could stay at a hotel, wash off the grime, order a five-star meal and sleep on a cloud-soft mattress.

'Have you?' he asked, low.

'Why do you think I didn't have enough energy bars? I had hundreds of them, boxes full when I came, and vitamins too—I spent all the money I'd earned on them. I fed the villagers to stop them feeding grass to their children. I fed them until the first harvest came through, and then the supply trucks made it past Sh'ellah's lines.' Her gaze didn't waver. 'You think you know about suffering? You have no idea.'

Her words shook him to his core. He'd known the suffering of loss—his parents had died when he was only nine, and Fadi's death three years ago had devastated him—but he'd never gone to bed with his belly aching for sustenance; he'd never known desperation to stay alive another day, or to save his children.

This was the most uncomfortable he'd ever been in a physical way.

He'd thought himself strong for not complaining about living on energy bars and travelling by foot all night—but he'd never been more wrong. Or more shamed with a few graphic words.

To hide the unaccustomed emotion, he broke the remains of the mouse-eaten energy bar in half, handing one piece to her. 'For what we are about to eat, I am truly grateful.'

She lifted hers in silent toasting, and ate.

'Oh, one thing,' he said in a conversational tone as he helped her pick up the plastic and ruined food. When she looked up, he smiled. 'Don't call me my lord. You know my name.'

The little smile vanished. 'We are what we are. You can run away from your life all you want, and tell people to call you Alim, but you're still the sheikh of Abbas al-Din. And no matter how many times you call me a dawn star, I'm the daughter of a miner.'

Burning fury filled him, but, tempered by long training, he was able to speak with careful restraint. 'Why is my brave saviour making excuses, hiding behind birth and titles?'

She shrugged. 'It's what people do. King or

sheikh, policeman or lawyer, rich or poor, imam or priest, father, mother, man and woman; it's who we are. They're roles assigned to us by the titles we bear, what we do with our lives.'

'What we do, yes—and what you do saves lives. So why are you putting yourself in chains, limiting yourself by birth? I don't expect you to be anything but who you are. I hope for the same from you.'

She sighed and kept her face averted, her eyes closed. 'It's not the same.'

'No, you're right, it isn't. You're protecting yourself from getting too close to me,' he said slowly, not knowing what he was going to say until he heard the words. 'We both chose to run from our reality and live this half-life, pretending that by saving others we can justify our past choices. If I am what I am, the same principle applies to you. No matter how far you run, you can't deny whatever it is that made you leave your family behind.' He gathered her hands into his and looked into her eyes. 'And no matter your status in life, to me, you'll always be a queen in my eyes, my Sahar Thurayya who saved my life, and made me a man again.'

For a moment she stared at him, and though he couldn't see it, he felt the blood pounding in her veins and her pupils dilating with the desire too intense and glowing to leave room for doubt. He was only holding her hands, and she wanted him...

So her words shocked him. 'My delusions might be thin, my lord, but they're all I have, and I'm not ready to let go of them. So please leave me to mine, and I'll leave you to yours.'

Simple words, yet they cut to his heart like the sharpest of scimitars, tearing at their desire and leaving it slashed and bloodied on the ground.

She turned back to cleaning the rubbish without a word. The shining, impish dawn star who'd made this hell of a journey the happiest time he'd known in years had withdrawn again, replaced by the quiet, uncommunicative woman of the first day.

Would he never learn to keep his thoughts to himself?

Coward, coward. The word rang in her head like a shrieking alarm, awakening her from this half-life, as he'd called it. *Pretending what we do justifies our past choices.*

Did he have any idea how much he'd hurt her?

He'd taken her hands so sweetly, arousing her as much as he terrified her; then he'd dissected her life choices like an emotional surgeon. Tearing her soul to shreds without knowing the reason why she'd run in the first place...and realisation hit her with the thought.

She wasn't falling in love with him; she *was* in love with him. God help her for the world's biggest idiot, she'd let her guard down and fallen for a man she could never have. A beautiful stranger whose soul she'd recognised in moments; a smile from her dreams. At the worst time she'd met her soulmate, all her fantasies come to life in one man...

You can never have him. You'll always be alone, she reminded herself in fierce pain, and huddled a little further away from the warm, living temptation just a touch away.

Hana tried her best to keep that distance every night as they travelled, but, oh, he made it so hard by staying only a step from her at all times, kept talking to her as if she were answering...and he kept *smiling*, making her want to step right into his arms...

Three interminable days later, when the thin crescent moon was high in the night sky, the creek bed that had served as their cover had widened and flattened to half-marshy ground and the worst of the desert had given way to thin, straggling bush, they finally reached the elusive water source.

She moved forward, out of the cover of the trees, but, too close as usual, he pulled her back. 'Wait.'

She frowned, then nodded as she saw the barbed wire stretching around the waterhole. A warlord had control, and someone was bound to be watching.

'We're out of water!' She'd been hoping for one miracle in their quest: an unguarded water source. 'What do we do now?'

Alim's grin was startling in the deep night. 'We rely on the trained ecological engineer to find water.'

She blinked. 'I thought you were a research chemist?'

'I took geology and environmental studies to balance the knowledge.' He moved back into the shadows of the trees. 'Look for the tallest tree here, where the shrubs are bunched closest together.'

With new respect for this ruler of her ancestral home who hadn't once complained on their desperate journey, who'd given help as much as he'd needed it, and who cared about the planet as well as fame and his country, she did as he asked.

'Quick and quiet as you can,' he whispered. 'I doubt the forest will be left unchecked all night. It's too tempting for enemies to hide in.' He grinned at her with dogged determination.

He was being strong for her; he knew she was falling down into despair. She nodded in shame and turned away, searching the foliage for where it was thickest.

She gasped when she almost tripped over him some minutes later. He was on the ground, digging hard and fast with his fingers beside a thick tree surrounded by bushy scrub. He shook his head when she was about to speak, and tipped his head in a western direction.

There were lights, and movement.

She fell to her knees and dug beside him in silence. The ground was damp, growing wetter by the moment.

'We don't have time for the dirt to settle. It'll be muddy, but drinkable,' he murmured against her ear as he filled a canteen with a cupped hand.

She shivered with the feel of his breath inside her skin. How could the tentative touches they'd shared feel so incredibly intimate? How did she want him so much all the time?

'Any water's good water,' she murmured. All

urge to celebrate their find had been smothered by the danger so close. And she kept digging.

'Move,' he whispered into her ear. 'They're coming. The bole of the tree over the other side's been emptied by honey-gatherers, and the bees are long gone.'

'The hole in the ground,' she whispered frantically. 'They'll know—'

'*Go.*'

Obeying the imperative command, she slipped into the tree. She watched as he covered the hole with all the branches and leaves scattered about, used a branch with leaves to clean off what footprints he could. She ached to help, but knew she'd only ruin his handiwork.

The lights and voices came closer. *Go, Alim, run!*

As if he heard her heart's cry he lifted his head, listening for a moment; then he stood on the branch and, with a mighty leap, he landed three feet up the nearest tree.

'What was that?' a voice cried in Swahili from not far away. 'I heard something.'

Alim shinned his way up the trunk of the tree, fast and quiet, his knees gripping the bole as his hands reached for a thick branch, the backpack slung across his shoulders. He moved so fast he was almost a blur in the night. As he jumped for the branch, he hung in the air for a moment; then he swung his legs up like a gymnast, and landed face down. He lay along the branch, making himself as flat as possible. He reached for the backpack and did something with it, what she couldn't see; but now the men wouldn't find him unless they shone a light on that particular branch of that one tree.

But they probably knew about the hole she crouched in. She held her breath, pushed her back hard against the hollowed-out wood, and waited.

The light seemed shockingly bright as half a dozen torches filled the small copse at once. 'It came from somewhere around here.'

Then a laugh came, followed by others, and she almost gasped in relief. She let the air out, taking in fresh and held it again before one of the men spoke. 'A branch fell, that's all.'

The others made fun of the man who'd called the noise, and after a quick sweep of the area they all moved off.

Soon, Hana heard the sound of a Jeep revving up and driving away—but as they'd done the day before, she stayed still, her thighs and calves cramping and shooting pains darting from her hips to shoulders. For long minutes she heard only the sound of a locust as it whirred from place to place in search of food.

'Hana, I've got the water. We need to leave.'

The whisper was startling in the silence. Hana jumped, and groaned with the pain it induced. Everything felt frozen.

'Hana,' he said again, and even in the hushed voice, she could hear his impatience.

'I can't move,' she whispered back in misery she couldn't hide. She was so *tired*.

She heard him mutter something, and then his head and shoulders appeared before her. 'You're cramped?'

She nodded, feeling ridiculous, a burden at the time she had to be strongest. 'I'm sorry.'

'Don't blame yourself. It was inevitable given the restricted diet we've been on, all the walking and running and where we've been sleeping.' His hands reached for her feet. 'Let me help.' He removed her shoes and socks, and, from their awkward positions, he used his fingers to massage her soles, her heels, her ankles.

And up…up, calves and knees and—*oh*… slowly he pulled her legs straight as he released her muscles from their bondage.

It was bliss. It was an angel's touch, soothing, freeing…arousing. It was symmetry and beauty beyond his poetic words, magic beyond anything the *Arabian Nights* could conjure, and not because he was a prince, a leader, but because he was *Alim*…because it was Alim's touch. Because it was Alim, who enjoyed both her teasing and her imperiousness, her laughter and her silence…Alim, who wanted her only to be herself in his presence.

The ache replacing her pain was languorous, and again she felt more feminine, more *alive* than she'd ever been. How ironic that a sheikh was the only man who'd ever made her feel glad to be a woman…

He'd half pulled her out of the hole before her back spasmed and she cried out in pain.

'Hush, Sahar Thurayya, I have you.' And his hands pulled her the rest of the way out of the hole. He turned her around so tenderly the pain was bearable, and his fingers worked their enchantment on her hip joints, her spine…

She leaned back, falling until her head rested against his chest. She wept in joy with the exquisite relief. 'Alim…ah, it's *wonderful*…' She heard herself moaning his name over and over.

The uncoiling of her muscles was almost as incredible as the more sensual awakening. She felt as if she could fly, yet she was chained, chained to him, and it wasn't frightening, it was perfect.

It was Alim, and she'd never felt so alive as when she was with him.

'Yes, my dawn star, it is…wonderful,' he murmured huskily in her ear. He was moving to her shoulders, his thumbs rubbing the rock-hard muscles beneath her shoulder blades. 'Lean on me. Trust me. I'll never hurt you.'

Something in the words made her heart stutter—but then those marvellous fingers moved to her neck, soothing, relaxing, arousing her anew. 'I love the way you talk to me,' she whispered as her head rolled around, luxurious freedom once more.

'I've never spoken to any woman this way before,' he murmured roughly, sounding surprised by the words. 'You inspire me.'

She turned her face, smiling at him, half drunk on the physical release of her singing muscles; intoxicated by his touch, by the way he made her feel. 'What a beautiful thing to say…especially to a woman who smells so bad she offends herself.' Her eyes twinkled.

He chuckled. 'I think I lost my olfactories with the   cigarette-mud infusion.' As if it were the most natural thing in the world to do, he kissed her forehead. 'And I must have lost my taste buds to those energy bars. I can't even taste the mud on your skin, just oats and raisins.'

She was asleep; she had to be. She was on the hot sands dreaming of her perfect man in a strange oasis. Alim couldn't be real, this incredible man who seemed to need her.

She'd always been a late bloomer. She'd waited until she was twenty-five to dream of her teen idol, The Racing Sheikh, and make him hers. Any moment now she'd wake up in Shellah-Akbar, with Malika shaking her awake, and the rounds of the day would face her, caring for the babies and children, cooking the foods their little stomachs could handle, treating the men and women whose hunger made their teeth weak...

Not ready to let go of her dream, she moaned and lifted her face to his. 'Alim...'

The lovely ache sitting low in her belly intensified when he whispered her name and lowered his mouth, hovering just above hers—

'Hana, we have to go now,' he murmured, his breath brushing her mouth like a caress.

Lost in desire and joy and hope, she took a few moments for his words to sink in. 'What?'

Then she noticed the light at the edge of the bush.

'There's a light over there. I think someone's left their Jeep unattended. We have one shot to get it.' He put her shoes on fast, shoving the socks in her pocket; then he helped her to her feet, hands beneath her armpits, holding her up. 'You okay?'

Feeling ashamed by her stupidity—how ridiculous was it to want him to kiss her and he was thinking of their welfare?—she nodded, and in silence bent to shoulder her backpack while he used a branch to eradicate all traces of their presence here.

She set off after him as fast and quiet as possible. He indicated for her to follow his steps. She saw the broken branches, the crackling-dry leaves on the path, and put her feet where his had been every time.

Alim was going faster, circling the edge of the copse away from the waterhole and back to where the light had been. Surrounded by enemies, night bordering on daylight, there was only one chance for them to get out of here: the biggest risk of all.

CHAPTER SIX

ALIM didn't have to tell Hana what to do. She followed him without argument when he took over for the sake of their safety, as she'd jokingly said she would.

A woman who could lead when necessary, yet handed over the reins without question when she knew someone had greater knowledge? Hana was a rare and strong woman...she was everything that his wife Elira had never been, despite Elira's high birth.

Hana was everything he didn't deserve—the happiness, the joy in living he'd taken from Fadi with a stupid dare of a bachelor party...

Don't blame yourself, had been Fadi's last whisper. But how could he not?

He stopped when they came to the thin end of the protecting little maze of bush. Hana, watching his every step, stopped behind him.

'What's the plan?' she whispered in his ear. 'Do we check for keys, or hot-wire it?'

'Both if necessary,' he whispered back, his gaze scanning the area. He scented danger like the changing scent of the wind.

'If it's me you're worried about, don't. I know how to run to the target. I was the naughty child in the family, and learned to bolt to the broken paling in the back fence to escape when my mother came at me with the wooden spoon.'

He turned his face, smiling at her. 'Somehow I can imagine that.'

She grinned, the mercurial imp that lifted his spirits smiling from her eyes, and he rejoiced. 'Which part? That I'm fast?'

'No, that you were the family rebel,' he retorted.

'Why would you think that about me? I've been so obedient to your every command.'

'Right,' he snorted softly. 'Stop making me laugh when we're in danger.'

'Let us joke and laugh, for this morning we could die,' she misquoted, her eyes twinkling like the morning star he called her.

It made him ache to kiss her—but that was his constant companion, had been from the moment he'd first seen her eyes. Whether that craving was friend or enemy he no longer cared. His feelings for Hana grew hour by hour, minute by minute, and he knew she desired him...

What? You find one woman who wants you, and it makes you forget everything you aren't?

She desired him after seeing his deformed body. It was a miracle in itself; he could barely get his mind around it. But when she looked at him like that, every other thought, even the self-hate, flew out of his mind, replaced only with the fast-beating heart, the aching body, the *hope*...

Can it, you fool; you need to save Hana. Having scanned the area as much as possible, he put out his hand. 'Give me your backpack.'

She handed it over, and drew deep breaths. 'Ready.'

There was no way to protect her now. He threw up a prayer for her—Allah's will be done with him, he didn't matter—and muttered, 'Keep as low as you can and zigzag.'

She nodded. 'On your count.'

On three he took off at a dead run for the Jeep, jumping from side to side in case of enemy fire. *Let it be open let it be open...*

He felt Hana beside him all the way as if she were his shadow, running and jumping left, right, left, right. She split from him at the Jeep's front, heading for the passenger side, accepting his driving skills could save their lives.

The driver's door was locked, and he cursed helplessly—but Hana yanked her side open and dived in, unlocking his door. 'No keys, can you hot-wire it?'

'I can try,' he muttered, wishing his training included less princely duties and more modern-day Aladdin techniques. 'Leave the doors open.'

Within two minutes the wires he was crossing had created no spark. He growled in frustration as he returned each wire to its place. 'I can't do any more. The wires I've taken out might not be in correctly. I can't risk the car not starting or they'll come looking for the cause.'

'Wait.' Hana was feeling inside the glove compartment, and beneath the console. 'Look for a spare key. In these dangerous times they'd need to keep one hidden.'

It was precious moments they didn't have, but there was no alternative. 'You look inside, I'll do the outside.' At least she'd be less exposed in there. He dived back out of the car, crawling beneath the engine, searching frantically.

A few minutes later, he wanted to shout in

triumph; from the passenger tyre shield he held aloft a key that had been taped to its inside.

He threw himself back into the driver's seat. 'Get your seat belt on.' He gunned the engine, put it in the lowest gear and took off, avoiding the mine-laden waterhole region and the bushy scrub, and heading for the sand hills.

Mere seconds passed before they heard shots. The third one blew out the rear window, sending shards of glass through the cabin. 'Get down, Hana,' he barked, keeping the gear low and upping the accelerator until the engine whined with the need to gear up. He'd done sand rallies before; this was the only way to manoeuvre the Jeep while going as fast as possible.

This was a chase that only his skill with driving, theirs with bullets, and the depth of the fuel tanks would determine.

He revved the Jeep to breaking point. It screamed in protest, but began the steep climb up the hill. 'Find some ballast if you can,' he shouted, 'any weight to put in the back and keep balance.'

Hana pulled off her belt and crawled over to the back as another shot hit the back door. She didn't scream, but said tersely, 'I can stay back there for a few—'

'*No.*' The single word contained all the authority he'd held in his life. 'Find something that won't blow up if it's shot.' *Or die,* he thought but didn't say.

'There are two twenty litre water containers!' Slowly, groaning with the exertion, she hefted one of them over the back. 'We can keep one back for drinking in case we make it.'

'*In case?* Are you impugning my driving skills, or maligning the water I found?' He tried to sound light, but he was too busy trying to get up the hill, searching for signs of harder terrain.

'Just keep driving,' she muttered. 'These taps aren't so easy to open.' She grabbed their backpacks. 'I'll refill the canteens with fresh water.'

She was right. They needed all the advantages they could get in this race of life and death.

'There are guns in the back,' she cried, sounding exultant.

'Can you shoot?' he shouted as he jerked the wheel left, avoiding more shots from the two Jeeps chasing them, two hundred metres behind, not yet on the hill. Somehow he doubted she could shoot. Saving life was Hana's thing.

'No,' she admitted, 'but I can try. If nothing else it might scare them off.'

'It might also blow a hole in our roof,' he yelled, hating to say it. 'Any change in balance forces me to adjust my driving to that, and we don't have time.'

'Okay.' She crawled back into the front seat, falling back to the middle section with a shocked cry as the jeep jerked with the forced low gear.

'Sorry,' he yelled over the whining engine.

'It's—okay.' The words were strained—too strained to be shock from the fall.

'You're injured.' It wasn't a question.

'Dislocated shoulder,' she said in a breathless voice. 'I can't climb back over.'

He cursed his stupidity. Fool, he'd been relying so much on her intelligence and resourcefulness over the past days he'd forgotten she wouldn't know how to compensate for his sudden driving changes. 'Stay on the floor. Lay with your injured shoulder upward.'

'All right.' A few moments later she said, in a voice laced with pain, 'Tell me when you need to jerk the car again.'

Not even a complaint when she must be in agony—that was his brave, beautiful dawn star. 'Now,' he yelled, and counted to three in his head before shifting the wheel left.

He couldn't hear her over the straining engine, but the adjustments she had to make as the Jeep moved must be making her light-headed. 'You okay?'

'Yup.' She didn't say more, which told him how hard it was for her to speak.

'I can't help you yet, Hana. Can you hang in there until we lose these clowns?'

'Y-yup. I'm good.' She could barely talk now, but she tried—and pride filled him. She was incredible, a woman in a thousand, a queen in a miner's daughter's skin.

More bullets hit the Jeep, but because he was driving up and in a zigzag fashion, he'd made it close to impossible to hit the tyres or fuel tank. He called to her before every adjustment he made, and counted to three each time. She was so quiet she might have passed out with the pain. Concern for her lifted his guilt and urgency to stop to higher levels.

Half a tank of fuel left. Even using precious stores to avoid the enemy and outrun them, he'd have enough fuel to reach his truck, if it was where Abdel had said it was, thirty kilometres northwest of their current position. If the truck was untouched still he had the satellite phone, and could call the pilot who came in three times a week from Nairobi. The four pilots on call had to answer the call to any aid worker in trouble. He could meet them while they were still far from the refugee camp—and he could save Hana.

Up one hill, down another, he shifted gears with the terrain, jerking the Jeep from side to side and over again, finding the strongest terrain for faster driving. This was the race of his life—to save his dawn star.

Hana hadn't let him down once, in all they'd been through. He wouldn't let her down now.

Hana came to with a cry of anguish, as pain more intense than any she'd ever known ripped through her entire body. She struggled to sit up, but something held her down.

'Lie still, Sahar Thurayya. I only have one pull to go—' Alim's hand on her left shoulder pinned her to the ground outside the Jeep, while the other had her injured arm, just below the armpit. By the position of the sun, it was early afternoon. 'Take a deep breath and try to relax. One, two—'

And he pulled her arm before he said *three*, before she could tense up in instinctive response to expected pain. She screamed as the *click* inside her body put tendons, bone and muscle back in their respective places; white cells poured into the injured parts to heal, causing swelling. She fell back to the ground, dragging in jerky breaths until the worst of the agony subsided, and the spinning in her head slowed. 'I'm sorry,' she whispered.

'Nothing to be sorry for,' he said in a neutral tone, wrapping the last of their rags around her body, tying above the shoulder in a makeshift sling. 'I'm sorry my driving put you in this pain, and I couldn't reset your arm before you woke up.'

'How long was I out of it?' she panted, feeling the world shifting beneath her again.

He held out two ibuprofen tablets, and put them in her mouth when she opened it. Then he gently lifted her in his arms and gave her water to swallow them. 'Almost two hours. I wish it had been in a bed.' He touched her face. 'You're the bravest woman I've ever known.'

The gentlest touch, made in compassion, and the earth shifted beneath her again. In her body's pain she was too weak to fight the desire, the longing.

'Alim...' The tiny moan was filled with the

longing she couldn't hide, longing so intense it outstripped even her pain.

He bent his face to hers, and she caught her breath. His lips brushed hers, soft, too soft. 'Soon,' he whispered, and she ached with the intimacy of his voice, the desire he didn't bother to hide, combined with the tenderness that broke her defences, already stretched as thin as a balloon. 'When you're safe, my dawn star, we'll have time to see where our hearts lead us. For now, it's my turn to take the lead. Trust me, Hana. I swear I'll save you.'

As he lifted her into his arms and laid her tenderly across the lowered passenger seat, she said softly, 'You've already saved me.'

'They're not far behind,' he replied in grim purpose. 'I had to stop, or your arm could have been permanently injured.' He pulled the seat belt on for her. 'I've rigged my jacket against the roof handle in a loop for you. When I say "now", use your good arm to hold yourself steady.' He roped the torn-and-tied sleeve of the jacket over her good wrist. 'Okay?'

She smiled at him, touched that he'd risked his life for the sake of her arm, when she could have waited longer for treatment...touched beyond measure that a man as important as Alim could put her before his needs. 'I'm good to go.'

His eyes shone—and she swallowed a lump in her throat, seeing the pride there: pride in her. 'Of course you are. That's my Hana.' He closed the passenger door and ran around to jump into the driver's seat. 'If we get lucky there'll be an afternoon wind to cover our tyre tracks; but I'll have to go as fast as possible. I'm going to try for second gear, to reduce engine noise…'

Unable to speak, she nodded. *My Hana*, he'd said…and in his arms, she'd felt so cherished.

In a daze of pain and exhaustion, she closed her eyes and allowed the dreams to come. They were insubstantial things that would wither when the real world returned, but if these sweet phantoms were all she could have, she'd cling to them for as long as she could.

He took off in low gear, building the engine up. The hum and whine of the engine was strangely soothing. She felt him trying to keep the jerks of the engine to a minimum, to save her from pain; and her heart, so long starved of such cherishing, overflowed in tender gratitude.

She didn't know when she slipped into sleep,

but when she opened her eyes, it was past night-fall. Alim was driving with no headlights, bumping over obstacles he couldn't see. She didn't have to ask why.

'Are you all right?' She pulled her good arm from the torn jacket to touch his hand.

'I'm fine.' He turned a face filled with strain to smile at her. 'You slept for six hours. Feeling better?'

She nodded. 'What's wrong?'

For answer, he passed a compass to her. 'Are you up to a little navigation? My eyes suffer from night strain—another reason I left the circuit—and my glasses are in the truck. Shifting my focus from the terrain to the compass is giving me a headache.'

'Of course I can navigate—but can't we stop for a minute for the ibuprofen?'

'You took the last of it for your shoulder.'

'I'm so sorry,' she cried. 'You're not yet over the concussion, and eye strain can—'

'Can it, Hana,' he interrupted, his voice warm with laughter. 'I'm the big, strong man in this scenario, in control, and feeling pretty good about it. Me Tarzan, you Jane, remember—so, Jane, I need to know what our current direction is.'

She grinned, and checked the compass. 'We're heading northwest, Lord Greystoke.'

He chuckled. 'What degree?'

She squinted at the compass, and told him.

'Put your arm back in the jacket, Hana. I need to adjust the Jeep. We're ten degrees off course.'

He didn't need to tell her why; he'd been letting her sleep. She threaded her arm through, tugged hard and nodded. 'Go.'

He turned the wheel hard towards the north. Hana gritted her teeth, but the pain was far less savage than she'd expected. The combination of muscles and bone being back in place, and the tight sling he'd fashioned for her, had promoted rapid healing.

Now her first concern was for him. 'You've been awake twenty-four hours, Alim. No wonder you have a headache. You need to rest, and we still have the willow bark.'

'What I need is coffee,' he said in grim humour. 'If you can pull that off for me, I'd be *really* grateful. A few days without it and my body's still in withdrawal.'

'You must be exhausted. Can't we—?'

'Not now. The afternoon winds were too minor to make a difference. We need to keep ahead.'

He jerked a thumb back. 'There's a dust cloud five or six kilometres back. If I can see theirs, they can see ours—and they can drive in shifts.'

She sighed. 'I could take my share of driving if I hadn't fallen.'

'If you want to help, talk to me. Keep me awake. Tell me something interesting.'

That took her aback. 'Such as?'

'All the down and dirty details of your life,' he said, but in a warm, teasing voice. 'What made you want to nurse in the Sahel, of all places?'

What would he think if she answered honestly? *It was as far removed from my life in Perth as possible, and too far out of Mukhtar's limited range of imagination in his search for me.* 'The Florence Nightingale effect,' she said, shrugging. 'I saw documentaries on Africa, the ads for Médecins Sans Frontières and CARE Australia. I wanted to help.'

'How long have you been in Africa?'

She stared out of the window, seeing nothing but blackness, and felt a tug of longing for the pretty, twinkling lights of the city against the Swan River in her beloved Perth. 'Five years.'

'How long did you live in Shellah-Akbar?'

'Six months.' Six short months, yet she'd been

there longer than anywhere else. She was always ready to disappear. Her superiors expected it, knew she was on the run from someone. Her stores of food and canteens, the burq'a she used but that she didn't attend the mosque, told everyone what she was, but they didn't ask questions. They reassigned her whenever she showed up at one of the refugee camps—always a different camp, and a village in another direction.

She'd hoped to remain at Shellah-Akbar longer. For the first time in a long time, she'd felt among friends. Despite Sh'ellah's interest in her, she'd felt part of the wider family with the villagers' unquestioning acceptance and friendship. She'd felt—almost safe.

'It's a good place to hide,' he commented in a thoughtful tone as he geared up to drive down a hill. She started, so closely did he mirror her thoughts.

She didn't answer him, couldn't without lies.

'Thank you,' he said gravely. 'I'm glad you couldn't lie to me.'

'I owe you better than that.' She blinked hard against the stinging in her eyes.

He put the pedal to the floor to ride up yet another hill. 'You owe me nothing, Hana…but you're not going to tell me your story, are you?'

It wasn't a question, so she didn't answer that, either.

'We should only be half an hour from the truck.'

She said awkwardly, 'That's good.' The sooner she got away from him, the sooner she could start her life over without these silly dreams.

'Have you been back to Abbas al-Din since you left as a child?' was his next question.

'Only twice.' Once for three months, during her sister Fatima's meeting with her future husband and during the time of their courtship and marriage; once to meet Latif. She'd still be there now, happily living with Latif in a house beside Fatima, if only—

'Did you like it?' he asked, oddly intense.

Out of nowhere she heard Mukhtar's last words to her, the night she knew she had to get out fast and never come back. *I have to get out of Abbas al-Din. You're my passage to a new life in Australia. Hate me all you want, I don't care. I'm still rich enough to give you a wonderful life, and to take care of your family. Latif won't have you now. Your family has accepted the marriage will happen. You will marry me, Hana!*

She shuddered, wondering if Mukhtar had managed to find a way out of the country without her; if Latif had found another wife—

'Was it so bad?'

She willed calm, even managed to smile at him. 'It has wonderful culture, some amazing beauty.' It certainly wasn't the fault of the country that one of its sons had run drugs through the family import-export business, and that he was good at covering it up. If she hadn't caught him making a deal when she'd come to visit Latif—

'How long has it been since you were there?' she asked, to turn the conversation.

He looked at her, his eyes like a blank wall she'd run into. 'You know, don't you? The world knows what happened.'

He'd left three years ago, and he'd never returned. He'd checked out of the hospital the day after Fadi's funeral, long before his graft surgeries were finished. According to news reports, he'd sent a letter asking his younger brother Harun to take his position.

'You must miss home. I know how much I miss Perth.' Awkward words; she cursed her clumsy mouth. So inadequate for all the pain he'd been through.

'So Australia is home to you?'

She shrugged at the deft turning of the subject.

'I grew up there. Perth is beautiful, isolated from the rest of the country. Like Abbas al-Din it has deserts all around, and spectacular beaches. It has similar seasons, too. Hot and hotter.' She grinned. 'I think we're a tad too far west again.'

He nodded. 'We had to avoid some bad territory—*now*,' he warned her of the Jeep's movement. She hung onto the loop. When he'd turned the Jeep, he asked, 'You feel Australian?'

Slowly, she said, 'Yes and no. It's an unusual experience, growing up between two diverse cultures.'

'I didn't spend much time in the West until I was a man,' he said thoughtfully. 'How was it for you?'

She bit the inside of her lip and thought about it. 'We spoke Arabic at home, and English everywhere else. We dressed modestly, but in Western clothing,' she said, feeling awkward. 'We were brought up to respect our faith and to live in peace with our neighbours, but we were still…different, you know?'

She shrugged again. 'I never quite knew who or what I was, but I was happy enough.' That was why her dad had encouraged her to return to Abbas al-Din, to meet Latif when she finished her nursing degree. Australia had been good to their family socially and financially, but her parents had wanted their children to know their home country and culture, and marry where they'd feel comfortable.

She'd gone into her engagement with eagerness. Latif was a gentle, kind man in his midthirties from a good family, successful and ready to become a husband. He'd listened to her, made her smile, and with Latif she had felt happy. And best of all, when he'd promised to respect her opinions and wishes, she had known she could believe him. She'd *liked* Latif, very much.

He didn't listen to me when I said Mukhtar was lying, she thought sadly, nostalgic for that happy time rather than for Latif himself.

'Do you know where you belong now?' Alim asked, breaking into her dark reverie.

'Does anyone?' She sighed and shrugged.

'Sometimes we can't be where we belong.'

The curt tone didn't hide the intensity of suffering beneath. Hana glanced at him, saw his jaw tensed, his eyes focused too hard on the way ahead. 'You can't go home until you've forgiven yourself for what happened to your brother.'

He turned to her, and what she saw now took

her breath away: turbulent, beautiful male, endless *anguish*. 'You can't go back, and I'm guessing you only let your family down. I took a good, potentially great leader from a nation before his time.'

'And what did you lose?' she asked, seeing the half-truth inside his words.

It was the untold halves that left them both here in Africa, half-people suffering inside everything left unsaid.

He geared down. 'Now.'

She held onto the loop again, knowing he wouldn't say more—unless she pushed him. 'Abbas al-Din lost a good man, a strong leader— but they survived, they moved on. You lost your brother, and you've given up on life.'

'Fadi was more than a good man or strong leader,' he snarled without warning. 'He was a father to Harun and me when our parents died, our guide and mentor. He taught me everything, was my dearest friend and closest confidant.' The next words came out twisted with self-hate, and she ached for him. 'You have no idea. Fadi's with me everywhere I go, a permanent reminder that it was my fault he died.'

And that, she suspected, was the first time

he'd said anything so emotional since Fadi's accident. 'Alim...'

'Don't tell me he'd hate to see me like this. I know he'd want me to become the ruler he'd have been.' He spoke right over her before she could say the words forming on her tongue. 'But I don't deserve to take his place—it'd be as if I walked on his grave and took his life from him a second time!'

'I see,' she said, after a long silence.

He frowned at her, but said nothing. Perhaps he feared opening a can of worms.

'I think I'd feel exactly the same.' She pointed ahead. 'Watch where you're going.'

He turned, saw the massive rock looming ahead, and corrected his direction. 'But?' he asked, with a grim awareness in his voice. 'There is a "but" hiding in there somewhere.'

She smiled at him. 'Yes, there is a "but". But— this is about more than your private grief and personal feelings. Abbas al-Din lost a good, strong leader—but it could have a leader who's learned from his mistakes, and learned compassion from suffering.'

'My brother Harun is all that,' he said, through gritted teeth. 'He did everything right, even married the princess Fadi was contracted to wed the week after the accident happened.'

Wondering why Fadi had so recklessly risked his life a week before his wedding, she touched his hand, gripping the wheel with whitened knuckles. 'I can't blame you for refusing. That was asking too much of you.'

He lifted a brow. 'Thanks for the absolution, Sahar Thurayya.'

The blatantly sarcastic words didn't hurt her; his grief was as raw as if it had happened yesterday. 'But—I still haven't finished my "but",' she added, smiling gently, 'did you ever *ask* Harun what he wanted, or did you take it for granted he'd do it all and better than you?'

A long silence followed. 'What is it you're not saying?'

She bit her lip. 'I understand why you don't watch news reports of home, but it's left you with a wrong supposition. Your brother Harun isn't doing as well as you suppose.'

At that he put his foot on the brake and ground the Jeep to a halt, leaving the engine running. He turned to her and said in a near-snarl, 'What's wrong with my brother?'

His pain, his guilt was so intense beneath the

façade of anger. She blew out air as she tried to think of a gentle way to say it. 'I'm in contact with a few aid workers from the region. Local gossip has it that Harun is ruling Abbas al-Din well—but the people want you back. And while Harun's doing his best for the country, and helped put the nation back on its feet after Fadi's death, he has no personal happiness of his own.'

'Why not?' he asked, his voice dark and grim. 'Amber's beautiful, a genuinely nice person, too—and don't tell me he doesn't like her. I saw it in his eyes when they met. He was crazy about her.'

She replied with a reluctant sigh. 'Perhaps he was—but how did she feel about having to marry the youngest brother within weeks of Fadi's death? Tradition would have stated that you marry her—isn't that right?'

She almost felt the tightness of Alim's jaw. 'Yes.' He didn't repeat himself. Marrying Amber would have been repulsive to him—as repulsive as marrying Mukhtar was to her, but for different reasons.

'Palace gossip says he and the princess Amber are far from happy. In three years they haven't been seen smiling at each other in the way of lovers, let alone touching. Her ladies swear

Harun doesn't visit her bedroom at night—' she lifted a hand as he scowled and opened his mouth '—and it's backed up by facts. In three years she hasn't fallen pregnant.' She paused to let him absorb the knowledge of his brother's marital unhappiness before she went on. 'If there isn't an heir soon, you know what will happen next.'

CHAPTER SEVEN

ALIM stared ahead at the empty-seeming darkness: as filled with pitfalls and boulders as Hana's conversation. He did indeed know what would come next: the sharks would begin circling, from other princely families in the region to neighbouring countries, to powerful Western corporations and nations with greedy eyes fixed on their oil and gas reserves.

And he knew everything Hana wasn't saying. Was Harun drowning beneath the load of responsibility he, Alim, had tossed on him by disappearing? Why wasn't he happy with the beautiful princess he'd—he'd been forced to wed?

For the first time Alim realised how selfish he'd been to leave his younger brother alone and grieving. Drowning in his own grief, he'd been blind to Harun's needs. As Hana had said so eloquently, he'd expected Harun to pick up the pieces of a shattered royal family and a nation on his behalf. He'd known serious, stable Harun would do the right thing, do a better job than he, Alim, ever could—right down to marrying the princess when he couldn't face it.

'Thank you for telling me,' he said, and couldn't help the terse anger in his voice. He only hoped she knew it wasn't directed at her, but a reckless, passionate young man who'd led a charmed life until the fateful day he'd talked Fadi into racing him.

'I hope it helps you make the right decision.' Hana looked out of the window into the empty night. She was leaving the decision to him.

They both knew there wasn't a decision to make. He had to go home, ask Harun what he wanted, to stay on as sheikh or not, to remain married to Amber or not. Maybe if he had a bit of time out, he and Amber could work it out—

Then he glanced in the rear-vision mirror, and gunned the engine again. 'And what happens next might come to us, and sooner than we think if we don't move. I should never have stopped the Jeep.'

Hana turned her face to the back window, and paled. 'They're close.'

'Four kilometres, maybe more,' he corrected

gently, cursing himself for scaring her. 'The dust looks closer than it is out here, in the darkness.'

She nodded, and didn't speak again for long minutes. Then she said in a strained voice, 'It wasn't my place to tell you about your brother.'

'Maybe it needed to be said. And maybe I needed to talk about it,' he replied, surprising himself with the realisation that what he'd said was true. She'd made him want to live again, to stop running, merely by telling him of the suffering his little brother endured on his behalf.

She was holding onto the broken jacket as if it were her only lifeline. 'Not to me, Alim. Don't ask me, don't confide in me. I can't even help myself out of my own mess.'

'Maybe you don't have to, Hana,' he said quietly. 'Maybe life, fate or God brought us together for a purpose. Maybe we can help each other.'

'What, we met for the express purpose of solving each other's problems?' she asked, with the same hard sarcasm he'd unleashed on her only minutes before.

He shrugged. 'I don't know. I'm no prophet.'

'And I'm no wise woman,' she retorted. 'I'm just a half-Arabic, half-Australian miner's daughter who doesn't even know where she belongs.'

The self-hate in her voice was like a hand shoved in his face. *Don't go there.* But somebody had to open that door and show her the monster in her personal cupboard wasn't as big or bad as she feared—

But this wasn't the time, and he wasn't the man for the job. He couldn't even frighten off his own monsters. Why would God send a man who was such an obvious failure at his life to teach Hana how to live hers?

He said quietly, 'Science and the Quran teach us that we're all one family, Hana, from common ancestry. So if you see a division between us, it's only wealth. The division of high or low birth exists only in your mind.' To lighten the mood—he could sense her inner struggle to not look back—he added, 'We all need to eat, drink, sleep and use the bathroom, no matter how much some of us pretend we don't.'

'I have to believe that after the past few days.' She grinned at him. 'My poor energy bars really affect you, don't they?'

He mock-frowned at her. 'My bodily functions are a state secret to be kept between us alone; but once we reach safety, I swear I'll never eat another energy bar.'

Her musical laughter came rippling from her throat, and he ached again: ached to touch her hand, to draw her close, look in her eyes and see the restless need in her again when he finally tasted her lips. When they weren't talking, the need grew to unbearable proportions.

Which was why he'd poked his nose into her life, and allowed her to step an inch inside his. It had come to this: anything to stop himself for another minute, another hour, because if he touched her again he'd lose control. He was still in exquisite pain from massaging her; touching her made him want far more than an hour's release. His fingers on her bare skin, hearing her murmur his name in feminine awakening... He almost groaned aloud thinking about it. How *beautiful* it was to caress her—it made him feel...whole. As if he'd come home.

Whatever had happened in Hana's past, he was the first man to truly arouse her. He couldn't doubt it after seeing the glimmering dawn of desire in her eyes when he'd cupped her cheek in his palm. Such a simple movement for such an unforgettable reaction. What he wouldn't give to see her face vivid and alive for him for the rest of his life!

He'd give anything…anything but his brother's happiness. He could do nothing, say nothing until he knew the direction of the rest of his life. If he *had* a life after this.

'Be grateful for my poor energy bars—they saved your life,' she mock-admonished him, willing to play the game, too, to stay away from his hot buttons.

'As grateful as you were for my muddy water?' he retorted, mimicking the motions of tossing water out the window, and she laughed again.

Neither of them looked back, but kept laughing and joking. Neither spoke aloud their belief that they'd be dead in less than an hour.

'We're not far from the truck, if I followed Abdel's instructions well enough.'

She nodded. 'This is a fairly deserted region, and the scrub is high to the right.' She pointed to a thick wall of darkness. 'It'd be easy to hide a truck inside it, so long as you don't mind the duco being scratched to Billy-o.'

He grinned at her. 'Scratched to what?'

She turned her face to his, filled with comical guilt. 'It's an Australian term. I've got no idea what its exact meaning is—think it means pretty bad?'

He chuckled. How often he'd laughed in her

company; far more than he had in the three years preceding it…and it no longer felt like a betrayal to Fadi that he could laugh. 'Knowing you has been an education,' he said gravely.

'I live to serve,' she replied, bowing her head with the same gravity. 'I strive not to be completely forgettable.'

I'll never forget you, he thought but didn't say. Even if he never saw her again after this adventure, she'd for ever shine in his memory like the star he'd named her. But he *would* see her again, at least once—he'd make certain of it. 'Maybe you're not completely forgettable—just a little bit,' he conceded in a drawl.

'Oh, thank you so much,' she retorted, trying not to laugh—and he smiled inside at the indignation flashing in her eyes. She gave away her feelings for him with everything she said, and everything she left unsaid.

'Hold on tight and keep your eyes open, Hana. We have to find the truck.' He swerved the wheel, and the Jeep turned hard right. 'Look for some kind of opening. If we hide in time, they might pass our tracks in the night.'

'There,' she cried seconds later, pointing. 'Let me out. There's a track to the left there, covered with branches, exactly as Abdel described it. I'll clear it for you.'

'It'll go faster if we both do it.' It would be useless to command her to stay in the Jeep. After hours of enforced rest, she was determined to pull her weight. 'Try to run where the tyres will make indents. It'll make for less cleaning later.' He stopped the Jeep, and they both ran for the track, clearing branches and rocks in their way. Clever Abdel had done all he could to make certain the truck wasn't found. 'Keep the debris close by. We need to replace it for cover.'

After a few minutes, when they'd cleared all they could, he said, 'Get in the Jeep, Hana. You can't cover our tracks without putting your shoulder out again.'

She made a sound of frustration. 'What can I do to help?'

'Can you drive the Jeep?' he asked tersely. 'Just drive straight inside without turning, keeping it in first gear, and stop when the back of the Jeep is about twenty feet in.' He picked up a branch covered in leaves as he spoke, and headed for the furthest point he dared, given the enemy was only a few kilometres behind now.

Hana jumped into the Jeep, driving it into the

opened track while Alim brushed traces of the
Jeep's tyres for a hundred feet, then trailed the
branch behind him as he ran inside the track.

'Alim,' she called urgently, 'I can see dust
rising behind us.'

'Wait.' He threw the debris back across the
track, covering their trail as best he could.
'That'll slow them down a bit,' he panted as he
jerked open the driver's door. He lifted her up
and over the gear stick to the passenger seat,
strapping her seat belt on. 'You'll need the loop
to hang onto if this gets bumpy.'

She pushed her arm through the torn jacket,
holding tight. 'Go.'

He took off as slow and quiet as he could to
minimise their dust cloud, praising God she'd
thought to keep the engine going; with the
enemy so close, starting the Jeep would surely
have attracted their attention. Hana thought of
things ahead of time, and didn't let her worst
fear turn to mind-numbing panic. She was a
woman he could rely on to be by his side
through the worst of times, not wailing or expecting him to save her.

He flicked a glance at her as he drove through
the pitch-black trail. In the reflected light of the

dashboard panel, she stared ahead with calm resolution. She looked ghostly, like a phantom of wisdom and strength in the night.

Even now, she didn't panic or make demands for him to hurry every few moments, knowing it would make him more on edge. Her tranquillity in this worst of situations, her good sense was something more than any physical beauty a woman could own. She was a woman in a million; he'd never find another woman like her; and when this was over—

'When this is over and we're safe, I'm going to marry you.'

And in her silence, his jaw dropped a little at the outright gall of the proposal. He'd meant to tell her how he felt—but his words had come out so blunt even he was shocked. He flicked another glance at her, and saw her fists were clenched; her cheeks were white and nostrils flared. He called himself all sorts of names for stupid. If he'd shocked himself, he'd stunned Hana.

Yet he'd never meant any words more. *Idiot*, why couldn't he have said something romantic and poetic, to soften her and win her over first? Well, why not? She loved it when he called her

Sahar Thurayya—if he told her he thought of her as a queen above any born to the title—he scrambled to get his thoughts in order—

'No.'

The single word was neither blunt nor stunned; it was final. Just that one word, yet it encompassed a world of rejection. Now, when it was too late and she'd rejected him, his mind turned calm and focused; he had the fight of his life on his hands, but that was okay. His agenda was out there, and at last he had a reason to make her speak. Or so he hoped. 'Why?'

After a few moments, she said, 'Just no.' But there was a telltale quiver in her voice.

'Would you marry me if I wasn't who I am?' he asked, though he knew the answer.

'N-no. You don't mean it.'

No longer a quiver; she was stammering her words. She *was* considering it.

'Yes, I do. I want to marry you.'

'Well, you can't.' Desperation laced her voice. Though she was sitting right beside him, she was bolting away in her mind and heart.

'Don't you think I deserve a reason, my dawn star?' he asked in Gulf Arabic; he'd noticed before that she became more emotional, more vulnerable in her native tongue, and when he called her by the name he loved.

'I can't give you one,' she said, in Arabic. 'Please, just stop.'

'You like me,' he went on, his mind clear, his aim on target. 'You like me as much as I like you.'

'I—yes.'

He kept the smile inside; the situation they were in was too serious to waste moments chalking up points. 'To like each other is a rare thing, far better and stronger than mere desire, and it lasts a lifetime. Yet you desire me as well, Sahar Thurayya—you ache for me as much as I ache for you.' He didn't make it a question; they both knew the truth.

'Please stop.' The words sounded raw, hurting. 'This is ridiculous. We have people trying to kill us, and you want to talk about this?'

'I know the danger we're in, Hana. And if they take us, kill us, this hour, this minute is the last we'll ever be alone together. So say it, my honest dawn star.' Gentle, remorseless. Dragging her out of emotional hiding.

'Yes, all right,' she snapped. 'There's no point hiding what you've already seen. When you smile at me, my heart soars. When you touch me,

I—I ache, something inside me starts burning and I can't think of anything else but you!'

He struggled against the joyous laughter bubbling up inside. Never had he heard an angrier declaration of a woman's yearning for him...and never had it meant so much. 'So is it my birth, my position that you don't like?'

He kept his gaze focused on the trail ahead, but his mind was completely on her. On doing this last thing for her, bringing her out of a hiding far more complex than his disappearance. On saving her, if he could. His plan to rescue her was done—and if the worst happened, she'd at least know how he felt about her.

After a long silence, she grated out, 'It's not a matter of what I like or don't like. You know I'm not suitable. The country would be in an uproar if you didn't marry someone who could bring diplomatic or financial advantage to them all. That's how it works.'

He did know—but he also knew how to fight it, to use his power and people's devotion to his advantage. But though he could see that wasn't the real issue, not yet. 'Yes, it seems that Harun and Amber know it, too—to their cost. Is that what you want for me?'

'No!' She sounded so frustrated he decided to take a chance.

'What's the real reason, Hana? What hurts you so much you can't even say it out loud?' he asked, with so much tenderness in his heart he saw her gulp and press her lips together.

'Stop it. Just get us to the truck.'

'There it is, right ahead of us.' He didn't press her further; she was almost at breaking point— and it told him what he meant to her. 'Let's go, and pray constantly there's an exit to this track, and they're not waiting at the end of it.'

Hana opened her door and grabbed her backpack with her undamaged hand, and ran for the truck without looking back. The stiffness of her spine was a clear *back off* species of its own.

Does she know how her body language gives away so many of her thoughts and emotions? He ran after her and threw himself in the truck. He found the keys in his backpack zip pocket and, after ensuring all the other entrances were double-locked, he started the truck. 'It won't be easy with the truck's tyres gone, but—'

And he cursed inside as he saw the fuel levels.

'What is it?'

He turned to her, knowing he couldn't protect

her now…but he knew what he had to do. 'We need to refill the fuel tank. I have twenty gallons and a hose in the back, but…'

'But it's time we don't have.' She searched his eyes for a moment, her face white. 'We're going to be taken, aren't we?'

'We're not done yet,' he said with grim purpose. 'We're not giving up.' And from beneath the console he pulled out his ace in the pack: a satellite phone. As he drove down the trail, he speed-dialled the first number on memory, and spoke quickly. 'Brian, it's Alim from the northern run. I need help. I'm with one of the aid nurses from Shellah-Akbar. She's injured and needs medical assistance—' He listened as the pilot interjected with a vital question for the help he needed. 'No, she's not a local; she's Australian. We escaped the village a few days ago and are currently sixty kilometres north-northwest of the village with Sh'ellah's men not far behind. We need to get out, and fast. Is anyone in the region?' He nodded at the answer, and said grimly, 'If it helps, my surname is El-Kanar. Yes, I'm *that* Alim El-Kanar.' He felt Hana's wondering gaze on him as he listened again. 'Thanks, Brian, we'll meet him there.' He disconnected and tossed her the phone. 'We're meeting the pilot in twenty minutes at a prearranged spot. We'll only have a minute to get away.'

'You're going back to your life,' was all she said.

'Yes.' He flicked a glance at her; her face was pale, and she hadn't touched the phone. 'In case this doesn't work out, would you like to call anyone, make your peace?'

It was a tradition in Abbas al-Din, to make peace as a final thing; it prepared the heart to meet their maker. Hana looked down at the phone, her face filled with a hunger so pitiful it wrenched at his gut; then she pushed it away. 'No.'

She sounded as final as she had in rejecting him, with the same desperate resolution. His poor dawn star; how she suffered for whatever happened to her in the past. How small and lonely she looked, shutting him out from helping her. How brave and beautiful, with mud and blood from multiple scratches encrusting her skin and mouth, her hair splitting and breaking from its plait, stiff with the dirt plastered through it, and a cap torn so badly spikes of hair pushed through. Just Hana…his woman, his queen, even if she rejected him for the rest of her life.

He didn't flinch from the tasks ahead of him. To save her he'd do anything, endure whatever he must. And save her he would—from this current situation, and from what held her in such invisible chains. He'd set her free, no matter what it took.

Here we go, he thought as he saw headlights at the end of the trail. Grimly he shoved the gear down and pressed a series of buttons: his own special modifications for attack and defence. 'Hang onto the roll bar,' was all he said to her, and floored the accelerator.

Hana gasped as they headed straight at the Jeep blocking the path. 'Alim, we can't possibly make it past—'

He laughed, hard and defiant. 'Who's The Racing Sheikh here? You have no idea what I can do with this baby. Just hang on and watch— and trust me.'

She lifted a brow and smiled back, her chin high. 'Bring it on, Your Lordship. I'm ready.'

The truck bumped hard as he kept pedal to the metal, slowly increasing speed, the engine revving hard and high. Shots fired, but only made cracking sounds on the double-reinforced bullet-proof glass he'd made at his private lab in the basement of his Kenyan house. Hana shrieked the first time and dived down, but soon re-emerged with the same *come-and-get-me* laugh he'd done a minute ago. And the truck gunned straight for the Jeep blocking the path, more than twice its size and with the massive spiked bars now protruding from the front and sides—

The warlord's men dived out the doors seconds before connection, screaming as they bolted to safety. More shots cracked the glass but it held. And the truck lifted high, higher, as the specially modified rims lifted up and over the Jeep, crushing it beneath its weight and the rollers he'd lowered between the front rims.

He heard the men shouting as they took off, and grinned.

'Is there anywhere they can damage us with their guns?' Hana asked, sounding awed.

He slashed the grin her way. 'Nope. Only a bazooka or bomb will break this baby. It must be frustrating for them with no tyres to shoot out, the fuel tank triple-lined with hard-coated plastic over reinforced steel and boxed in lead casing, and bulletproof glass. They'll have to surround the truck to stop us.'

'They obviously don't have bazookas or

bombs. And if they do surround us, we can run them over.' She sounded excited, gripping his arm instead of the roll bars.

Good, she hadn't thought about the fuel situation. He didn't want her to remember, just as he didn't tell her that the rubber rims on the tyres had only been made to last a hundred ks at most. By the time they ran out she'd be safe—that was all he wanted. He drawled, 'Is this enough excitement for you, my dawn star?'

She laughed. 'My parents would say this was my destiny. I was born to be killed in a shoot-out or car chase. They could never stop me watching those kinds of shows or reading suspense novels.'

It was the first time she'd mentioned her family without pain—but he didn't have time to pursue it. 'Here they come. Four Jeeps, about a hundred metres back. They're probably waiting for reinforcements to arrive before taking on the truck.'

'They won't be able to surround the truck before we reach the plane.' She sounded exultant. 'We've done it, Alim. *You've* done it!'

He fought to keep the sense of inevitability from his voice as he replied, 'No, we did it.' He revved the truck to its limits before changing gear. 'This is going to get rough.'

She held to the roll cage as he took the straightest route, right over rocks and on shifting sand and dirt. She bumped and lifted right off the seat so many times, her shoulder had to be in agony, but she didn't make a sound, except when he asked her to check the GPS built into the console, to be sure they were still heading in the right direction. Nor did she look back.

There was a blinking light to the west, only a hundred feet up and falling when they drew near to the assigned meeting place. The enemy was only five hundred metres behind.

He put the headlights on high beam and flashed the old distress call in Morse code, as prearranged: CQD. Then he geared down and stopped. 'Hurry, Hana. We only have seconds.'

She nodded and grabbed at the backpacks. 'Leave them,' he said as he opened her door for her, rough with the exhaustion hitting him, almost thirty-six hours awake. 'Plane weight has to be kept to a minimum.'

She nodded and took the hand he held to her, stumbling at a dead run for the Cessna.

The small plane hit ground and skidded as it twisted to avoid the truck. The second it was still, the door flew open. 'Get in,' the pilot yelled, but Alim had already scooped Hana into his arms, and was putting her in. 'Go.'

Hana's eyes widened as she saw it was only a two-seater plane; the back was loaded to the ceiling, with no time to unload to make room for him. She struggled against the pilot as he strapped her in. 'No, Alim, you can't do this!'

'Go!' He slammed the door shut, hardening himself against the sight of her anguished face, the hands against the windows, as if she could reach him from behind the invisible barrier.

Swirling dust covered him as the plane began to move. Red dust choked him from behind as the warlord's men arrived.

'Alim, don't do this! *Alim!*' she screamed through the Perspex, hitting it with her fist. Tears rained down her face, his brave Hana who never cried or complained. *'Alim!'*

'I'm coming back for you, you hear me? I'll find you, Hana,' he yelled to her, with such conviction even he almost believed it.

The plane took off on a short run as the Jeeps screeched past Alim, aiming their rifles high, ready to shoot them down—

'My name is Alim El-Kanar,' he announced in Gulf Arabic, calm, imperious in all his mud and torn clothing. Praying one of them knew enough Gulf Arabic to get the gist before somebody killed him. 'I'm the missing sheikh of Abbas al-Din. I am worth at least fifty million US dollars in ransom to your warlord.'

It seemed they all understood well enough. Twenty assault rifles dropped from the skyward aim, and levelled at his chest.

CHAPTER EIGHT

Compassion For Humanity Refugee Camp,
North-western Kenya
Nine days later

'HANA, you're wanted in Sam's office,' one of the nurses called to her as she passed, bearing a box of ampoules for immunising babies. 'Looks like your transfer's come through.'

'Thanks.' She put down the box, and headed for the director's office, sick with relief. Soon she'd be out of here, in a remote village where there was no radio blaring in the main tent, replaying the ongoing story of The Racing Sheikh and his capture by the warlord Sh'ellah, demanding a hundred million US dollars for Alim's safe release. In the village she wouldn't see newspapers with pictures of him as he was released two days before, so tired, with bruises on his face and arms that showed how brutal his stay with the warlord had been.

Everywhere she went, aid workers talked about him. Who'd have known? Sure, they never saw his face—he always hid it behind the full flowing scarves of an Arab man—but the quiet, withdrawn driver was The Racing Sheikh?

Women lamented missing out on a chance with him. Men wished they'd gone out in that *wicked* truck of his to see his skills firsthand. And Hana moved around the camp like a lonely ghost, waiting, waiting for word from him, for his voice…

I'm coming back for you… I'll find you, Hana.

It obviously wasn't going to happen. He was the sheikh again. He had a life that could never include her.

She walked through the flap—

'You have the burq'a on again.'

The air caught in her lungs as her diaphragm seized up. Slowly she turned towards the main desk, hardly daring to believe—but he was there, he was *there*, standing by the side of the desk, and smiling at her as if it had been only hours since he'd seen her. Smiling as if she was something beautiful and special to him.

'You're out of hiding, I'm back in it,' she

said, when she could speak. Pulling the veil from her face, her hair, without even thinking about why she did…knowing they were alone without even checking.

He made a rueful face. 'I'm clean at least.'

'You look different without the mud.' One step, another, and they were only inches apart—which of them was moving? She thought it was her, but she was in front of him too fast, shaking and gulping back more foolish tears. 'You're here.'

His smile was tender; his gaze roamed her face. 'I told you I'd come for you.' He added, 'Sam's gone for ten minutes. Any longer and someone could come in and find us.'

Hana barely heard him; she shook her head, mumbling, moving to him, 'They hurt you…' Her hands were on his face, trembling, drinking in his skin, warm, living skin—he was alive, *alive*. And she was crying again. 'Alim, I was so scared—' She put her hand over his heart, felt it beating. 'You're alive, *alive*.'

'I'm alive,' he agreed, still smiling with all that emotion shimmering in those dark-forest eyes. His fingers reached out, touched her cheek. Beauty ripping through her, stealing her soul with a touch.

Then without warning her bunched fist hit him, attacking without power, as weak as the knees buckling beneath her. 'You frightened me half to death,' she sobbed, collapsing against his chest and his arms enfolded her for the first time. 'I couldn't eat, couldn't sleep for worrying. How could you risk your life like that, Alim? How *could* you?'

'For you, it was for you,' he murmured into her hair. 'For my beautiful, brave dawn star, I'd sacrifice more than my freedom for a week.'

'Don't risk yourself for me, I'm not worth it,' she whispered, tears raining down her face, aching for him. 'You could have died, Alim! Your country needs you!'

'Not as much as I need you.'

Simple words, stealing her breath. She stared at him, her eyes asking the questions her heart dared not risk.

He glanced at the watch on his wrist. Its understated magnificence stood between them like the fire-wielding angels barring the way to paradise; it must have cost more than she made in all the five years she'd been here. 'The plane's waiting. We have to go, Hana.'

A rock fell on her chest, constricting breath.

'I—I understand.' She wheeled away before he saw the devastation in her eyes.

'I don't think so. A delegation from the UN wants to speak to us about our experience, to know about the new borders and Sh'ellah's weaponry and acts against people in the region. They'll be at my house in Mombasa tomorrow.'

Joy streaked through her at the same moment as panic. She'd be with Alim again, if only for a short while. Where the UN went, so did the media. 'I can't!'

He gathered her hands in his. 'I agreed to it on the condition that your face and identity were kept out of it. You have my word I'll keep your identity out of any interview. But what we say could help the people of Sh'ellah's region escape from his violent domination.'

'Oh.' She felt small-spirited and petty standing before him, thinking of herself when the people she cared about still suffered far more than she ever had. Hating that she still couldn't face her reality…and that, too soon, she had to tell Alim the truth of why she couldn't marry him, or be his lover. 'Of course,' she said, hiding the shivering inside. 'I'll get my things.'

'Your things are already in the plane,' he said,

adding when she stiffened, 'Neither of us has a choice, Hana. Sam's going to tell those who ask that you've been reassigned, so there's no connection between us anyone could take to the media. I've spoken of the nurse that saved my life, of course, but you're still safely obscure.'

Strange, but, though he'd spoken without inflection, when he said 'safely obscure' she felt like the most miserable of cowards. 'Thank you.' She lifted her chin, refusing to apologise for or explain her life choices.

'There's a car right behind the tent. I have to ask you to walk to the front of the camp while I ride there, so if I'm recognised entering the car, we aren't seen together.'

She nodded and, realising too late that she still had her hands on his chest, blushed and dropped them. 'That's fine.'

'We'll talk in the plane, Hana.' His eyes glittered with soft meaning.

'All right.' She all but bolted from the room.

The director, Sam, had done his job well. At least six people wished her well at her new assignment as she headed for the gates, and she felt like a miserable liar. What was the difference? Wasn't that what she'd been the past five years?

I can't make myself lie to Alim. And that terrified her, given the ordeal facing her.

The car wasn't fancy or designed to draw attention, she noted in relief as the back door opened, and she hopped in. The windows were tinted, and Alim sat in the furthest corner from the people milling around in front of the gates. The dark glass between the driver and passengers was pulled up, creating a sense of intimacy.

The car took off, purring with the quiet smoothness that screamed *expensive.* 'Not quite as loud as the truck or the Jeep,' she commented, aiming for lightness, her heart pounding hard at the look in his eyes.

He shook his head, moving closer to her. 'It's twenty minutes' drive to the plane. I never said hello before.' He tipped up her face and, before she could react, pulled aside the veil she'd replaced after leaving the office, and brushed his mouth over hers, soft, lingering, too soon over. 'Hello, Sahar Thurayya. I've missed you...as you can probably tell.'

Her pulse beat so fast in her throat; she couldn't make her tongue move or her mouth open. Their first real kiss...so gentle and chaste—he was treating her with the honour of—

She closed her eyes. Despair washed through her like a river's surge, leaving her entire body feeling unclean in the wake of arousal she had no right to feel. One kiss, and she was so alive, so vivid and aching for him—but she could never have him, not as husband or lover. She gulped down the pain in her throat, but still couldn't speak. All she could do was shake her head.

'No?' he asked softly. 'You didn't miss me? It's hard to believe, given the greeting you gave me.' The fingers at her chin caressed her skin. She shivered with the power of his simplest touch, chains far stronger than any Mukhtar could shackle on her. 'Look at me, Hana.'

Long moments passed, but the pain only grew worse as she hesitated. She lifted her lashes.

'I know you said it doesn't revolt you, but that was in a life-and-death situation. This time, I want you to look carefully.' He pulled his light linen shirt over his head, leaving his chest and stomach bare—revealing the pinkish grafts over twisted scars running across one shoulder, half his chest and down over his stomach. 'More surgery will help but there's only so much anyone can do for such extensive second-degree burns. I'm trusting that the nurse in you will be able to refrain from feeling physically ill at the sight of me,' he said, with a wryness that tore at her heart. 'I have scars on my thighs as well, since some of the graft skin came from there when a couple of the other patches didn't take.'

She didn't have to ask where the rest of his skin came from. *Fadi's with me everywhere I go,* he'd said. Yes, his pride and his pain in one, the eternal reminder of his loss; he did have Fadi with him wherever he went. His brother's dead body had been his donor.

More tears rushed up, useless, bittersweet longing and empathy. Her trembling fingers touched his ruined skin, almost feeling the flame that had destroyed his clean flesh. Her fingers drank in the proof of survival against the odds. Oh, the agony he must have suffered!

His hands covered hers. 'Do you find me revolting—not as a nurse, but as a woman?' he said, guttural. 'If so, it ends here. I'm for ever in your debt, Hana. What happens from here is in your hands. My future rests with you.'

She heard nothing after the word 'revolting'. She pulled her hands out from under his, and the quivering grew as she touched him, yearning and pain intertwined. She didn't realise she'd moved forward, falling into him, until her lips touched the mangled scars on his shoulder, her tears mixing salt to the warmth. And once she'd started, she couldn't stop; it was beautiful, so unutterably exquisite that the thought of not touching him, not kissing him, was agony. She must, she *had* to kiss him again...

'Alim,' she whispered, the ache intensifying, a woman's hollow throbbing of need for her man, unfamiliar and beautiful and addictive. She kissed the skin of his throat, chest and shoulder again and again, her mouth roaming over what he was now, what he'd always been, and both filled her with the deep anguish of feminine need, because his suffering had shaped him into the man she loved. 'Alim, Alim.' Breathless voice filled with the restlessness of desire unleashed, her hands growing fevered in intensity of wanting.

His hands lifted her face. 'No, no,' she mumbled in incoherent protest, palms and fingers still caressing him. 'No, more, I need more...'

Then she saw his eyes, lashes spiky with tears unshed. 'My Hana,' he said, husky. 'My sweet, healing star, you've sealed our destiny.'

With a cry she pulled him to her, falling

backward, his aroused body landing on hers as their lips met. Her fingers twined through his hair, caressed his neck, moving against him and moaning in need, wanting more of him, so much more. So many years feeling half dead, living only for others, existing inside the shadows of fear; now she was alive at last. More kisses, deep and tender, growing more passionate by the moment, and, oh, at last she knew how it felt to be filled with love given and returned…

The car pulled up. Loud engine noises came from outside. They were at the airstrip. He was hovering just above her, smiling in such tenderness her heart splintered, and she came back to a sense of herself—who she was; *what* she was.

What she'd done to him…and to herself.

The happiness shining in his face shattered in silence. He helped her to sit up, tossed the shirt over his head before the door opened. She shoved the veil back in place, eyes lowered, mouth—foolish, needing mouth—pushed hard together to stop words tumbling out. Not yet, not yet. On the plane. In Mombasa. Anywhere but here and now.

The plane was a small jet, pure luxury in appointments. She'd never seen anything like it.

Strapped into her seat beside him, she looked out of the window, waiting for him to speak, to ask the questions. Praying that, from somewhere deep inside, she'd find the strength to tell him.

They were in the sky before he spoke. 'If I know you, you went straight back to work when you arrived at the camp, right?'

He sounded so ordinary. He was teasing her a little. It was a gift; he was moving past the awkwardness and embarrassment, allowing her time, letting her tell her story when she was ready. And she felt a smile form at the opening; she couldn't stop it. 'Well, I did shower and change. Not the best thing for open wounds or sick people, all that mud.'

'It wouldn't inspire much confidence in your hand-washing methods.'

She chuckled. It felt surprisingly good, the banter. With Alim, she could be herself, be teasing, silly Hana, and he liked it. 'You should have seen people's faces as I walked in. A friend stopped me from coming in, thinking I was a refugee, so dirty and everything crumpled.'

'You definitely smell better now.' He inhaled close to her. 'No lavender though. What is that?' he asked, sounding nostalgic, as if he missed the lavender—and she resolved to wear it again before she could stop the thought. Foolish woman, wanting to please him.

'Spiced vanilla. A local soap made from goat's milk. You know, Fair Trade and all that. The locals bring carts in and sell to whoever they can.'

'They must be doing well to be able to afford the scent.'

'The director got the original makers in touch with the Fair Trade organisation, and first sales were so good they began branching out into scented soaps. The whole village is part of the industry now.'

'I wonder if we can get Shellah-Akbar interested in some similar kind of project.'

'They have a new nurse,' she said, sadness touching her. She missed her friends, the sense of accomplishment at seeing babies grow; the serenity of having, not somewhere to hide, but somewhere to belong.

'I've had preliminary reports from the region. Sh'ellah's not happy, even with the money from my ransom.'

Her stomach thudded. She knew what that meant: he'd been looking forward to having her, and would take it out on whoever he could. 'Is everyone all right?'

He covered her clenched fist with his hand, opening it and threading his fingers through hers. 'Don't worry, Hana. I told my brother they helped save my life, the risks they took to cover our traces.' He added, 'Harun visited the five villages in the region yesterday. He gave them the choice of ongoing protection or a new home in Abbas al-Din, their own village in a safe, arable area under the sheikh's personal protection. Given Sh'ellah's rampages, many of them have chosen to come. Harun's negotiating with the government to look the other way while our special forces evacuate them.'

In a region where 'negotiating' meant millions changing hands, she wondered how much they were paying to save these people who should mean nothing to them. She held tight to his hand, even knowing she shouldn't. 'Thank you,' she choked.

'My brother is a good man, and a strong ruler.' He bent to kiss her knuckles. 'There are advantages to marrying me, Sahar Thurayya,' he murmured, between husky and teasing. 'You'll find more as we go along.'

The shock of his words ran through her, his agenda out in the open when she wasn't ready for it. She dragged in a breath, pulled her hand from his and then said it, hard and blunt. 'I can't marry you, Alim.'

'Why not?' he asked, calmly enough. 'Don't say you don't love me, Hana, not after the way you kissed me in the car. I won't believe it.'

Her stomach knotted; her diaphragm jerked, and she had to hiccup the words. 'I'm already married.'

CHAPTER NINE

A HOLE opened up beneath him, sucking down all his hopes and dreams. Alim stared at the only woman he'd ever loved, thought of all the sacrifices he'd made for her sake, how she'd risked her life for him. 'You led me to believe you were a widow.' The tradition was for the sheikh to wed a highborn virgin like Amber—but given the choice he intended to present the people, he'd believed they'd accept her, accept his marriage. But now…

'I know.' So tiny, her voice, filled with shame.

'You said you had no husband. You said that!'

She made a frustrated sound. 'I don't.'

'What?' He shook his head, trying to clear it; it felt as if the mud he'd washed off two days before had entered his brain. 'You either have a husband or you don't.'

She wouldn't look at him. 'I was married by proxy. I disappeared before they could force me to marry him, and I never returned. So I'm married, but I don't have a husband.' Her mouth twisted, and she mock-bowed. 'Bet you've never met a five-years-married virgin before.'

His mind raced with the information even as his sense of betrayal grew. 'You danced around the truth. You led me to believe you were free!'

'You asked the first day. You were a stranger. What did you expect, my life story?' Flat words hit him like a slap, locking him out.

'When I proposed to you—'

'Stated your intention, you mean,' she retorted with a hard laugh. 'You never asked me, never proposed...my lord Sheikh.'

He felt his nostrils flare at the goading title. 'Okay, so it wasn't the most romantic proposal, but saving your life was taking up my energy at the time. I thought you'd understand.'

'Oh, I understand. Yet another male knows what he wants, and I'm expected to fall into line, just like Mukhtar! He ruined my engagement to his own brother to cover up what he'd done. He thought marrying me by force would buy my silence. So he told my father and Latif that I'd *seduced him.*' She pressed her lips together, and wheeled away. 'So I'm married, thanks to the

El-Kanar family's male-oriented laws that allow them to buy and sell their daughters like dogs or cattle—and I'm a whore for touching you.'

Alim didn't need the dots connected to see the picture. His anger against her, his sense of betrayal withered and died; he saw her manic laughter the other day in its true light. It truly was *ironic*, as she'd said. He'd accused her of seducing him, just as Mukhtar had, yet she was still a virgin.

When he could recover his voice, he said, 'Your fiancé believed his brother?'

She nodded.

'And your family?' he asked, the diffidence unfeigned.

She shrugged. 'Mukhtar told his family. The scandal devastated my parents, stopped me marrying elsewhere, and ruined my younger sister's chances of finding a good husband. To save Fatima, Dad went along with Mukhtar's plan. A woman can't testify against her husband in Abbas al-Din,' she finished in bitter mockery.

Dear God in heaven, what a mess, Alim thought. In Abbas al-Din society, if Hana didn't marry the man she'd supposedly slept with, she'd be shunned—and the news would reach the community in Australia long before she could return there. So rather than marry a man she despised, she'd chosen to live as an outcast—but she'd lost everything.

No wonder she'd reacted so harshly to his slightest dictum, or mocked him for taking the lead. No wonder she'd turned him down flat for announcing their marriage as a fait accompli…

His mind raced to find a solution for her, his saviour, his love. Aching to reach out, to draw her against him and let her know she wasn't alone, he asked, 'Do you know where they are? Your family, and Mukhtar?'

If anything, her back stiffened more. 'I know you want to help me, but if he finds out where I am…even you can't interfere between husband and wife.'

The thought of her as Mukhtar's wife through lies and treachery sent fury flooding through him, a primal urge to find him and take him apart, piece by piece…but that was the last thing Hana needed right now. Only practical action could help her—and she had no idea of what he could do. 'What is it you hold over him?'

She shook her head. 'He's family now. Exposing him destroys my family.'

Moved by her loyalty in the face of so much loss, he reached out to her, let his hand fall. She didn't need his love, she needed—

She needs a miracle, he thought grimly. It was a tangle past unravelling—but he had enough of the puzzle pieces to try to pull at the threads, and see what fell. She hadn't contacted any of her family in five years; she could only be going by what she knew then, a girl on the run.

He said the only thing he could say without causing her further suffering. 'All right, Hana. I understand. I won't pressure you any further.'

After a long stretch of quiet, she said huskily, 'Thank you.'

She was crying in silence, and, bound by his promise, he couldn't reach out to her. They sat inches but miles apart. He ached to comfort her, his silence the only gift he could give.

He'd had such plans for tonight...but now he had other plans to make.

'This isn't a good idea,' she said as she entered Alim's house in Mombasa as the sun began to set. The wide glass doors to the balcony had a gorgeous beach view onto the Indian Ocean, the warm breeze rustling through the palms lining the sand. The crashing of the waves felt like her heart, constantly pushing its tide against the immovable earth of her situation.

The table was set for two, with candles and soft lighting...

'I've arranged for your accommodation in a bed and breakfast down the road.' Though the words were expressionless, her gaze flew to his face. 'Your reputation is precious to me,' he said quietly. 'As for all this—' his jaw tightened '—I ordered it when I believed we'd be engaged tonight. We might as well eat, and there are two chaperones here. My staff will never tell anyone you were here—and they'll take you to your accommodation when the meal's over.'

What could she say? He was putting her needs above his, and wasn't blaming her for the ruin of his hopes. 'All right.' The words felt choked. 'Alim, I—I am sorry.'

His eyes softened as he seated her at the table, removing her veil with such tender hands she wanted to cry. 'You have nothing to be sorry for.'

He'd stopped calling her *my star*. He hadn't called her anything at all since he'd stopped fighting for what never existed in the first place. He barely touched her, and when he thought she wasn't looking his eyes darkened with pain. He'd accepted it was over, before it had even begun— and, irrationally, she felt like screaming. *Aren't you going to fight for me?*

Even if Mukhtar didn't exist, Alim could never marry the daughter of a miner—and she couldn't become his lover. It would destroy her family, and, no matter what they'd done, she loved them. They were good people, even if they'd put worry about what their world would think above her needs, and tried to hush up what they saw as their daughter's shame.

The meal was delicious, rice and curries of the region, lamb and fish with potatoes and traditional spices, and fried plantain. It was a shame neither of them ate much, only using food as an excuse to be quiet.

Soft music played from the CD, ballads that fitted the sunset, so soft and pretty from this south-eastern beach. After a while, Alim pushed his chair back. 'This is ridiculous,' he said, with a violent touch.

'Yes,' she agreed, relieved to be saying something, anything.

'I can't pretend like this.'

'I should go,' she said, soft, sad.

'No.' He'd pulled back her chair and had her in his arms before she could move away. 'Don't go,' he murmured, his cheek rough against hers. 'I hate being with you knowing I can't have you, but being without you is worse.'

She ached to wrap herself around him, to share the kisses of this afternoon; but the time had gone, the words *I'm married* had made everything real. 'This only makes things harder.'

He held her tighter. 'Things have changed in my country. Proxy marriages have been illegal in Abbas al-Din since Fadi's rule. I don't know if your father knew that—'

She closed her eyes when they burned. 'Even if that's true, I can't repudiate the marriage after all these years. It would humiliate Dad.'

'He ruined you.' The words were filled with fury. 'And don't you think your running away from the marriage he'd organised for you shamed him publicly, embarrassed the entire family? Don't you think clearing this matter will be better for them all?'

'He'll never forgive me,' she whispered. 'That's why I can never go back. And you—you need a suitable wife, a princess who knows how to help you.' She pulled back to look into his face, his beloved face, one last time. 'Please, just let me go.'

'I won't let you go, not knowing you live in hiding, never planning beyond your next escape—' He held her shoulders, his eyes blazing. 'Come to Abbas al-Din. I'll buy you a house, and we can...'

'I can't be your mistress,' she murmured, broken. 'It would destroy my family's good name. I can't hurt them that way after everything else.'

'You're the one who's suffered because of them,' he snarled. 'After what they did to you, you care so much?'

She shivered and moved closer to him, burrowing into him as if the night were cold. 'I thought I didn't. I want to hate them, but I can't. I can't—I have two sisters and a brother who are innocent of anything against me.'

Alim's mind raced like his cars around the circuits. 'Then we'll marry here in Africa. We can stay here.'

'No!' she cried. 'You can't renounce your position for me. I'd always be the woman who stole the sheikh from his people—and my family would be humiliated again.'

'So they're more important to you than what we have?' he grated out. 'Or are you just making excuses to leave me? Was the way you kissed me in the car just a sham, a nice goodbye to the infatuated freak?'

'*Don't.*' She pushed at his chest. 'I'm doing this for you. You know how much I feel for you—but this can't work. I'm the wrong woman for you!'

'You think any woman of high birth is what's best for me?' Finally he released her. 'You know I married a princess once, right? It was a nightmare. They said she died of a rare form of pneumonia—but the truth is Elira killed herself after the doctors said she couldn't bear the sons the nation needed from her. She was the perfect wife in public—but unstable, highly emotional in private, always screaming and crying, wanting what I couldn't give. In three short years she drove me nearly insane, Hana. I won't marry for reasons of state again.'

The words were so cold, bitter, she shuddered again. 'Not all princesses are like that, surely?' She tried to laugh—but he moved away, his eyes blank. 'We had a semi-affair of a week's standing. A few touches, a few kisses, can't become the love of a lifetime,' she went on, trying to smile, to be brave for his sake.

He interrupted her noble sacrifice with words dripping with ice. 'I'm thirty-seven, not a raw boy. I know what I want. I want you. If you won't marry me because I'm a sheikh, I won't be one. Harun's become an outstanding ruler anyway—the people only want me because I was once famous. If you won't marry me, I'll live alone.'

How could a heart soar and crash at the same time? She didn't know whether to laugh or cry. 'Sooner or later, you'll surely find a suitable woman you can…love—'

'Will *you*?'

The savage words threw her into confusion. 'Of course not, I've told you I can't—'

'If he was dead, would you come to me—or would you find someone else? A suitable man— what is that to you?'

She shivered at his freezing tone. 'I'd go home,' she said quietly.

'And find someone else?' he pushed in a snarl. 'Would you?'

She shrugged helplessly. How could she *stand* another man to touch her after what she'd shared with him? Brief moments, enough to live a lifetime remembering…

'Tell me, Hana. Say the words just once.'

A raw command filled with all the betrayed hurt he wasn't ashamed to show her. She gulped and looked at the floor. 'I shouldn't.'

'Hana, it's all I'm asking of you—well, all I'm asking it seems you *can* give me,' he amended, with such painful honesty her heart melted. 'You made no vows to Mukhtar, so you won't betray your father; but only tell me if it's the truth—if your kisses were real, if your desire for me was true. If it wasn't, just walk out now and you'll never see me again.'

Alim was right: the vows made hadn't been *her* vows; she hadn't made them. Alim's pain melted her wavering resolution. Why not tell him how she felt, just one time?

She couldn't look at him as she said words she'd never said to any man. 'I love you,' she said softly, and joy so poignant it hurt her soul spread through her, shining from within. Then she looked up into his eyes, glowing with bliss stronger, more lovely and heartbreaking for its being only for tonight. 'I love you, Alim, I love you.'

His eyes were full of anguished love. How well

he knew her; he knew she was saying goodbye. 'I love you, Hana.' He pulled her into his arms, and all that was cold and dead in her came to beautiful life. 'I love you.' And he kissed her.

Shouldn't, wouldn't, couldn't all went out the window as she threw her arms around him and deepened the kiss to beautiful, pure passion that sent dark memories of Mukhtar's one attempt to arouse her spinning to the mental garbage. This didn't make her feel shamed or dirty, because it was Alim…

She felt him removing the rest of the burq'a to reveal her plain cotton skirt, rose-hued shirt and sandals as she wound a hand into his hair, the other holding him tight at his waist. She loosened his shirt and slid her hand beneath, palms and fingers drinking in the man she loved. 'Ah,' she cried as his mouth trailed over her jaw, her ear, shivering with a primal force growing with each time they touched. 'Alim, say it one more time, call me your star.'

'I love you, Sahar Thurayya,' he whispered in her ear. 'My bright, beautiful dawn star, you lit me up when I was hiding in the darkness, you made me a man again.'

Clinging to him, whispering clumsy words to

him of her love, she felt the change begin, her joy fail. Their love was like the dawn star he'd compared her to: seen for a brief, shining moment, lighting her life like the morning sky, but it was impossible to hold within her hands. She was a beggar maid to his king, a gutter snipe to his poet. This wasn't real love; it was grati-tude for saving him, she knew that…but that he even *thought* he loved her now was her life's private treasure. It had to be enough, because it was all she could have.

'I have to go,' she muttered as his kisses grew so frantic she knew it was now or never—and for his sake it had to be never.

'Stay with me tonight,' he murmured against her throat, hot, rough, demanding.

She shivered again, fighting temptation with all she had. 'I can't,' she whispered, feeling a jolt of pain rush through her as she took her hands from him. 'Please don't,' she cut in when he began to speak. 'It will only make things worse.'

She had to cut the connection while there was a chance he'd get over it. He had to produce heirs for the sake of his nation—and she wasn't kidding herself that he'd love her for ever. She knew she wasn't unforgettable by the way Latif had left her life at a speed faster than Alim could create in his best Formula One car.

The passion died in his eyes, but the love, the care for her, grew stronger. 'If he finds you, Hana…do you want that to be your first time? Or will he do worse to you to protect himself?'

She wheeled away. If he knew what she believed Mukhtar would do to her, no force on earth would stop him from trying to protect her from him. 'I'll be fine. I promise.'

'You can't promise. In the Russian-roulette life you live, there'll always be another Mukhtar, another Sh'ellah.' His voice was harsh, but not aimed at her. 'Come back with me to Abbas al-Din. I swear you'll be happy—and I couldn't be otherwise if you're near me.'

The lure of happiness pulled at her heart and soul, poor, helpless fish—but the hook he dangled with the lure was a killer. 'I'll be fine. I survived twenty-six years before I met you—' she forced the teasing twinkle into her eyes '— I'm fairly sure I can stumble through the days, aft…' The words dried up, and she closed her eyes. She couldn't say it. *After you're gone.*

'For thirty-seven years I tried everything the world could offer, education, travel, excitement—and my heart wasn't in anything, Hana. Then I met you and it was as if I crammed an entire lifetime into a few days. Strangers' souls entwined for ever, my star. What we feel is for life, whether you believe it now or not.' He turned her back to him, caressing her arms as he looked into her eyes. 'This isn't over. I won't let it be over. I won't let you hide from me.'

She blinked hard, but the tears welled up faster than she could control them. 'It has to be over. Please don't ask me again.' She hiccupped on the last word.

His thumbs brushed her cheeks; his mouth followed, kissing her tears away, and more fell. 'I mean it, Hana. This isn't over. I'll find a way for us. You have my heart, my wise, cheeky star, you bring light and love to my life. I refuse to endure life without you.' He smiled down at her, as strong as he was tender, and another hiccup escaped her, a half-controlled sob of loss. His arms enfolded her. She snuggled in, trying to catch her breath, to stop her throat *hurting* so badly.

'You're tired. I'll call Yandi to take you to your accommodation,' he murmured, after a long time had passed, and the music on the CD player had faltered to silence.

She nodded against his shoulder. Alim helped her back into her burq'a, her old friend and shield that had begun to feel like her enemy, symbolising all she was leaving behind. Again.

When Yandi was waiting outside the house for her, Alim held the door open, and she almost ran through it. At the top stair of the wide balcony leading to the night-flooded beach, she turned for a moment. Taking her last look at him.

'It's not over. I'll find a way for us,' he said, low and intense.

She shook her head. 'Go home. Be the man you were always meant to become. And—and be happy, Alim. I need you to be happy.'

She fled down the stairs before she could do something stupid, like tell him she'd changed her mind, she'd do anything to be with him another day. Another moment.

CHAPTER TEN

The next afternoon

THE female UN delegate looked directly at Hana. Alim could see she wanted to squirm every time one of them paid attention to her. She'd sat through the interview for three hours in silence unless someone asked her something directly. 'Hana, you did a brave thing in saving Sheikh El-Kanar. If you ever need help with anything, please call me.' She handed her a card.

'Thank you,' she said yet again, and rose. The need to get away, to hide once again was so strong on her face, he wondered if they could all see it. 'I'll leave you all now.'

With ten long strides he caught up to her in the doorway. 'Hana.'

She gave a silent, mirthless laugh as she turned at the outside door. 'I don't know if I'd have been more disappointed or relieved if you hadn't followed me.'

'I told you we're not over,' he said, gently pushing her outside the door, closing it behind him. The sun shone brightly on them both; the warm breeze caressed them.

'Please stop,' she whispered with an anguished glance around, to see who watched. 'We can't do this, Alim, you know we can't.'

His eyes blazed, but he spoke gently. 'I made a few calls last night. There are things you need to know.' He pulled a thick roll of paper from his jacket without ceremony.

Her gaze lifted, searched his for a moment. Slowly she took the paper from his hand.

'I hereby find the marriage ceremony between Mukhtar Said and Hana al-Sud, signed by Malik al-Sud on behalf of his daughter Hana al-Sud, to be illegal according to Amendment 1904 of the year 2001 by The Supreme Ruler of beloved Memory, Sheikh Fadi El-Kanar, and therefore declare the marriage to be void. Signed, Mahet Raad, Supreme Justice of the nation of Abbas al-Din.'

She read the document aloud in Gulf Arabic in a dazed voice. Eyes glazed with shock stared into his. 'The marriage is void? But how…Alim, I told you—my family…?'

'I found Mukhtar,' he replied grimly. 'He was persuaded to give me a written confession to his lies, and the deception he practised on your father and the imam. He'd forged your signature on a betrothal agreement, so they'd believe the marriage was legal.' He held out a second piece of paper, Mukhtar's confession. He didn't tell her about Latif's heartfelt apologies. He didn't want any ghosts between them.

When she finished reading the second paper, her hand lifted unsteadily to her forehead. 'Alim…I'm *free*?'

Her other hand reached out to him. He took it in his, again feeling the inexplicable sense of homecoming. 'You're free, Sahar Thurayya. Free to do whatever you wish.'

Her eyes darkened; she shook her head. 'But…my family? Do they know?'

'They know,' he said grimly. 'They're waiting to see you. You're coming to Abbas al-Din with me—' he checked his watch '—in five hours.'

Her hand gripped his, her eyes dazed. 'What? I—I didn't hear you…' She swayed.

Alim cursed himself, and scooped her into his

arms. 'Too many shocks in a few minutes.' He opened the door and, without looking to see if the assemblage of people inside his house watched them, he carried her into a spare room, laying her down on the bed. He removed the veil that was her shield, her protection against the world, and caressed her cheek. 'I took your strength for granted, my star. Rest here until it's time to go.'

Eyes huge with uncertainty stared up at him. 'What did you say before?'

She really hadn't heard him. He sat on a chair by the bed, taking her hand in his. 'I got all the information within hours—Mukhtar's escape plan failed when you left, and he ended up in prison. He was persuaded to tell the truth in exchange for a transfer to a lower-security facility.' He didn't mention the hours of haggling negotiation with Mukhtar's lawyer as Mukhtar tried to gain freedom in exchange for his confession. Instead he moved to the point he knew really interested her. 'I talked to your father last night, Hana. They're in Abbas al-Din now, visiting your sister. They know you told them the truth. Any more is their story to tell— but they want to see you. We fly out in five hours.'

A shiver raced through her. She looked

anything but happy. Slowly she shook her head.
'No.' The word quivered, but sounded final.

'No to what?' he asked, frowning. His mind
was sieving through mud right now after a sleep-
less night arranging for Hana's freedom.

'No to everything.' She turned her face from
him. 'I need to go.'

'No, damn it, you don't. You're not running
away again, Hana. I won't let you play the
coward,' Alim snarled, losing it without
warning—and she stared up at him, her eyes
huge, and filled with the strangest mixture of
uncertainty, stubbornness…and intrigue.

Exultation shot through him. She *wanted* to
say yes, he could feel it—and she was respond-
ing to his fury with interest instead of in mockery.
Hana would never accept orders—unless she
trusted him, wanted and loved him enough to
hope there could be a future for them…

But one thing was painfully obvious to him: if
she was thinking of a life together, she wasn't
ready to admit it. He'd known that last night
even as she'd said *I love you*. She might want a
future with him, but she didn't believe in it. But
if she came to Abbas al-Din with him, he was
hoping to show her that, again, her deepest fear

was over. It existed only now in her mind, like the monster in her childhood cupboard.

'You've faced and passed the hardest tests on earth the past five years—so why are you being such a coward now?' He purposely kept his voice hard. 'You're free of Mukhtar, free of the chains holding you. Your family made the wrong decision, and yes, they hurt you—but you love them. It's time to stop running from them. It's time you forgave them.'

'You don't understand,' she muttered, a frown between her brows.

'You say that to *me*?' He laughed in her face, pushing her away to bring her closer. 'Do you have any idea how hard it was to face Harun, knowing what I've put him through in the past three years? Yet he paid my ransom without thinking twice, and came to meet me the hour I was released.' He lifted her chin. 'At least your family deserved your distrust. I deserved for him to let me die at Sh'ellah's hand.'

Her lashes fluttered down, reminding him of the hour they'd met—it was the only time she'd hidden her real self from him. Secrets, yes, but never had she hidden the person she was. 'I'm not ready for this.'

'You think I was ready to face Harun? Yet I was the one at fault, needing his forgiveness,' he demanded, his caressing finger beneath her chin at odds with his uncompromising tone. 'So tell me, Hana—when will you be ready to forgive them? Would you like to pick a day when you'll finally feel brave enough to do the right thing?'

'When would you have been ready, if the circumstances hadn't forced you into it?' Her cheeks blazed with colour; her lashes lifted to reveal eyes as aroused as they were furious.

She was consumed with desire, because of a simple movement of his finger, and a plan flashed into his mind.

Acting on it, he laughed in her face. 'What circumstances? You mean that I *chose* to save your life and risk my own for you? Or do you mean that I announced my name and offered a ransom so you could get away safely? Are they the *circumstances* that forced me?'

Her mouth set in a stubborn line.

He shrugged. 'I'm calling your bluff, Hana. Come back with me, or I tell your family how you've been risking your life for five years rather than face them—and then I'll send them to you. You know I can,' he growled as she stared up at him in mingled desire, fury and resentment. 'This is going to happen, so accept it and move on.' Before she could argue he bent and kissed her, deep and hard, gathering her close. He wasn't above using any means possible to convince her to come with him. She needed reconciliation with her family as much as he'd needed to face Harun and apologise for the nightmare he'd created of his brother's life by disappearing.

Half expecting a rebuff, or for her to lie stiff and cold beneath him, he felt jubilation soar when she moaned and wound her arms around his neck, meeting his passion with blazing flame. She arched against his body, moving in delicious friction, her hands in his hair, caressing him with ardent eagerness. Oh, how she wanted him! All her slumbering fire belonged to him—and he'd do almost anything to keep it that way for the rest of their lives.

For now, though, he had no promises he could make her; he didn't know yet what his future held, or what place she'd take in it. But there'd be nothing, no future for them if he couldn't even make her come to Abbas al-Din with him.

It felt as if he ripped his heart from his chest

as he pulled away. 'We leave in five hours,' he snarled, but his fingers trailed slowly down her throat, across her shoulder, and he saw her quiver again. He wanted to shout in joy for the heady knowledge of how badly she desired him. 'Sleep for an hour or two; you'll need it. When you wake, we'll walk on the beach and talk.'

Heavy-lidded eyes lifted to his, aching with as much painful wanting as anger, and he knew he'd won the battle—she'd come to Abbas al-Din, and face her family—but on the issue of marrying him, the war was far from over.

It was another incredible sunset, softer than the rich, rioting colours in western-facing Perth, but the soft rose tipped the foaming waves, and the palm trees lining the beach caught the rustling-soft breeze. A star winked at them from low in the sky, the first of the night.

'It's so beautiful, isn't it?' Hana murmured, awed, forgetting her fury with him for a moment. 'Africa's a place of such amazing contrasts. There's so much beauty and faith, as well as the war and suffering.'

'It's the same as anywhere else, with the same people, good and bad,' Alim replied. 'Oil in

Nigeria, gold and diamonds in South Africa, Mali and Mozambique bring the greed. But the beauty—' He took her hand in his—she revelled in the simple connection to him, had been wondering why he hadn't touched her during the half-hour they'd been walking—and said, softly, 'The unique beauty of Africa is why I keep coming back. It—gives me rest.'

You give me rest.

The thought flew out of nowhere—or maybe it came from everywhere, everything he'd been to her. She'd never had a friend who could laugh with her and let her be herself; a man who listened to her and wasn't too arrogant to learn from a woman; a man whose smallest smile made her day, whose touch, who cared enough to give her a compelling honesty that brought her out of emotional hiding, and face her cowardice. He'd looked inside her turbulent soul and calmed the storms; he brought her from a state of darkest cynicism to trust, tenderness and, unbelievably, forgiveness.

If she'd brought him *back* to life, he'd *given* her life. She could be what she'd always wanted to be: a normal woman, wearing rolled-up trousers and shirt, barefoot and holding hands with the man she—she—

Couldn't resist, couldn't turn from, could barely say no to.

And that was why she was going to Abbas al-Din. He'd literally kissed her into capitulation. Far more than merely desiring him, or liking him, she *needed* him. She loved him, had to be where he was. It was as simple as that— and as impossible.

Impossible was never more obvious than today, with so many reminders all around him, the armed guards keeping a discreet distance. His current location might be secret, but it wouldn't take the media long to find out—and they'd want to know who she was. How long would it take them to find out? A day, a week? *Drug runner's ex-wife is our sheikh's saviour…*

Tonight, here on the beach, in the jet, would be their last hours alone together—and she intended to cherish them, even if they were surrounded by armed minders all the way.

They might as well flash a neon sign; *Go home, low life, you can never have him.*

'I can see why you love Mombasa,' she finally replied, her fatalism and her love tearing her heart in two. *Run. Run as far and fast as you can…don't leave him, now or ever…*

'I'm keeping the house,' he said quietly. 'The family of my housekeeper will look after the house while I'm gone, and I've given them the cottage out back to live in permanently.' He led her around a late surfer who'd just flopped on his towel. 'You've taught me to look outside myself, Hana. I thought being here, helping, was enough to justify my existence, and I could keep my life, my*self*, separate. I know now I can't, and I don't want to.'

Wonderful words, yet they sounded like a farewell, even before they boarded the jet. Yet he was smiling… Her gaze riveted to his mouth, her lips tingling and her body aching, she managed to say, 'I didn't do anything.'

Still with that tender smile curving his mouth he stopped, turned her around. Her heart pounded like the waves against the sand as he bent to her. The kiss was soft, sweet, perfect…and too soon over. 'You're like that,' he murmured, pointing at that low-slung star, 'like the story of those men who were led to the Christian Messiah. I was lost in the darkness of self-hate, and you showed me the way to redemption, to joy in living, without even knowing you did it.'

She couldn't help it, couldn't stop herself from

lifting up on her toes, kissing him again—and then again. 'You did the same for me,' she whispered. 'You saved me.'

'We saved each other.' He rested his forehead against hers, and she adored the intimacy of it while still aching for more. 'Face the truth: we're souls entwined, Sahar Thurayya. We need each other.'

Yes, their souls were entwined, and as far as she was concerned they always would be; but how could she believe this was anything but a lovely fantasy, a romantic idyll she'd treasure when she left him? When they reached Abbas al-Din, everything would change. She'd have family responsibilities again, and Alim would discover he *was* a sheikh, his country needed him—and he'd need a woman who could be a helpmate, a queen in every sense. And when that happened she'd let him go with a smile, doing her best not to show her life was over.

But for now he was Alim, the man whose soul was inextricably part of hers, who'd quietly reached inside her and taken her heart before she'd known it was gone. So she smiled back and murmured, 'Yes,' not wanting the dream to end. Not yet.

He moved his cheek against hers. 'One day

you'll believe in us, my star,' he murmured in her ear, making her shiver. 'Maybe when we're married ten years and have seven children.'

Uncomfortable with his perception, how finely tuned he was to her emotions, she laughed. 'Hey, you want seven kids, you can give birth to them. I sure won't be going past four.'

He chuckled, and kissed her cheek. 'Four it is, then…so long as at least one of them is a cheeky girl who shows the boys how to not take themselves so seriously.' When she didn't answer— her throat had seized up with longing and useless dreams—he checked his watch, and made a smothered exclamation. 'We need to head to the airstrip.' Turning quickly, still holding her hand, he led her back towards the house.

When they arrived everything was already packed and in the sleek limousine—and the beautifully attired driver winced when Alim opened the door for her. 'I'm too messy,' she protested, reluctant to enter this gorgeous vehicle in rolled-up trousers and vest top, with bare, sandy feet and mussed hair. 'Is there a garden hose here? I can wash it off, and not dirty the car.'

'No need for that.' Alim frowned at the driver, who immediately apologised gravely for any embarrassment he'd caused her, and offered to fetch her a towel, which made her feel worse. She whispered, almost squirming, 'He shouldn't have to clean up after me. It's not right. It isn't as if I'm anyone important.' With a lowered gaze she walked to Alim's front garden and turned on the tap, washing off the sand.

'See what I mean?' Alim's laughing, rueful voice sounded right behind her, and she started, turning to him. 'You teach me by example to not be so arrogant.' He shoved his feet beneath the water, rinsing off and turning the tap off.

'It's your car, you can do as you want,' she mumbled, feeling her blush grow.

'Yes, I can, and I would have, but for you.' He lifted her hand to his cheek, cradling it, and she forgot all about the watching chauffeur, his minders, the state of her hair or anything else. 'You consider everyone. It's something I've never had to do. Our parents trained us to treat all people as equals, and our position means we serve the people, but some lessons need a brush-up.' He kissed her palm.

Even as her eyes grew heavy and her body swayed towards him everything they'd been through suddenly overwhelmed her, and she needed—needed him. 'Alim,' she whispered.

He saw it; his eyes darkened. 'I'm all yours once we're in the car, Sahar Thurayya.'

Without thinking she turned and bolted for the limousine, and hopped in without waiting for the driver to hand her in. When Alim joined her, she barely waited for the door to close before she threw herself into his arms. 'Hold me,' she whispered.

The limousine took off smoothly, and the passion in his eyes gentled as he drew her closer, up into his lap. He held her close for a long time. 'It's been a hard time for you.'

She nodded into his shoulder. 'I thought you were going to die when they took you—and then you come to me, but covered in bruises. They hurt you for my sake, Abbas al-Din loses millions to save me because you sacrificed yourself for me…and then, then you give me back my family, my freedom…' She hiccupped.

'Give me a chance; I'll be everything you ever want or need, my star,' he murmured into her hair. 'I can even give you a happily ever after— but not with a prince. A simple sheikh will have to do for you.'

Simple? In a top-of-the-line limousine, about

to board a first-class jet? She choked back a giggle. 'Just call me Cinderella? I'm more like the little matchstick girl.'

Alim tipped up her face, his eyes full of tenderness at her deliberate roughening of her voice. 'Do you see your ending as tragic as hers was? Need it be?'

All her smart cracks withered under the tender fire of his questions. He saw too much. 'Maybe not tragic,' she conceded, 'I just don't see the whole palace-and-prince/sheikh thing. It was never part of my dreams.'

He stilled, and she felt the question without his asking. 'I dreamed of a man who came home to me at night, played chess or Scrabble or backgammon, and held me as we watched the news, and played with the kids and occasionally brought home dinner when I was tired,' she said quietly. 'All I ever wanted was an average guy who could accept me as I am.'

'You can have all that,' he replied, just as quiet, caressing her shoulder. 'I've never tried to change you, Hana, only circumstances around you, for your sake.' He lifted her chin, and kissed her lips. 'I'd move mountains if it would make you happy.'

'You already have,' she whispered. That was what made it so hard. How could she have all her dreams come true in a man whose life gave her nightmares? 'But average? It's something you can never be.' *In any way,* she thought, sadness piercing her.

'I can. I have been for the past three years, Hana.' He caressed her hair, and love swamped her. 'If Harun is happy to continue as the sheikh, we can return here and—' He frowned as she shook her head. 'I realise that now the world knows where I've been it'll be harder, but we could find another area that needs our combined skills.'

'It's useless,' she said sadly. 'You know it, Alim. People will know you...and they'll sell your whereabouts for money. I can't blame them for that—but your life would become a circus. Face it, you had one shot at disappearing, and you did it well—but it'll never work again.'

'Then we start our own aid programme, and run it as ourselves. I'm a multimillionaire in my own right, from my racing days. We can live comfortably enough even if I gave ninety per cent of it away.' Then, as she sighed and shook her head again, he said, 'Don't tell me you don't love me, Hana. I know you do.'

Unutterably weary, she climbed off his lap. 'I haven't had one good night's sleep in two weeks, Alim. I'm tired, I feel numb and scared and in about two hours I have to face my family, the family I still don't know how to forgive, and you're asking me to change my life for you.'

Alim stilled. 'Actually, it's me constantly offering to change my life for you,' he said harshly. 'You don't seem willing to give an inch. I guess that shows what I mean to you beyond desire. I guess it shows what those three words last night were worth to you. Was it anything more than a nice goodbye to you, Hana? Is what you feel just not worth the fight?'

Shame heated her cheeks. 'We're at the airstrip,' she mumbled.

He climbed out of the car, and handed her out with grave courtesy, as if she were a dignitary instead of an aid nurse with bare feet and sand in her trousers. They walked up the red carpet and into the jet, a barefoot sheikh and his Raggedy Ann saviour, in silence.

CHAPTER ELEVEN

ALIM watched in grim empathy as Hana grew paler, her fingers twitching more with every movement of the jet towards Abbas al-Din.

He'd forced her into this, and now he was facing the consequences in her silent misery. As she'd told him, she wasn't ready to face a family pitifully eager to ask forgiveness, to make amends for the five years of unbearable loneliness and pain they'd caused her.

How could they possibly make amends? Even if Hana found forgiveness for them in her heart, how could she ever trust them again?

Then he noticed his own foot was tapping against the ground. He had to wonder if Harun could ever trust him again, either. He'd let his brother down as badly as Hana's family had done to her. He'd even, by his desertion, forced Harun to marry a woman he, Alim, hadn't been able to face as his wife. Harun had found no happiness with Amber, and that was Alim's fault, too.

God help them both, this surely had to be a worse homecoming than the fabled prodigal son ever endured.

When a servant brought their bags with changes of clothing and shoes, Hana thanked the woman gravely and then walked into the gold-fitted bathroom without a word to him. She emerged in a beautiful ankle-length skirt the shade of sunrise, and a creamy long-sleeved shirt embroidered with tiny beads that shimmered as she walked. Plain sandals adorned her feet. Her hair was braided back. She wore no jewellery or make-up. She took his breath away.

She didn't look at him as she sat, put her seat belt back on, and her hands and feet began twitching again. He came back from his change in the gold-and-scarlet attire expected—

Of what? A prodigal brother, a runaway sheikh?

She flicked a glanced at him, and her eyes slid down to her clothes, so simple and modest.

He felt the distance growing between them without a word spoken.

I'm still Alim, he wanted to shout; *look at me, touch me, I still breathe and hurt.* He'd thought her the one person who could look beyond appearances, and see him.

It seemed he'd never been more wrong.

As the jet began its descent Hana struggled not to throw up. The duality of love and betrayal, longing and anger tore her heart into shreds.

A hand touched hers, stilling the tremors. 'It'll be okay, Hana.'

Glad of an excuse to relieve hours of bottled-up anguish, she turned on him. 'Are you telling that to me, or yourself? Look to your own reunion with your brother and the wife that should have been yours, because you know nothing of how I'm feeling right now!'

He turned his face away. 'How can I know what you keep locked away from me? Your heart is like a tap that keeps switching from hot to cold, burning and freezing me.'

Her head, already buzzing, felt as if a swarm of bees inhabited it, but she sat straight and proud in her seat. She had enough to think about without letting the shame in. He'd saved her life, made this reunion possible, had erased Mukhtar from her life, and—

'I'm just trying to make the farewell easier,' she

whispered so soft he wouldn't hear, wanting to lay her arms on the flight table, her forehead on her arms; but then he'd know how weak and needing she was, how she longed for his comfort.

And that would wrinkle his silken magnificence.

Too soon, the jet made its descent, landing, and then they walked along another red carpet into another limousine—Alim must have asked for no welcoming party, for which she was grateful—and the whisper-quiet saloon purred towards the palace.

As they drove through the streets Hana shrank further down into the seat. No one seemed to know Alim was back; there was no fanfare, no cheering crowds, yet still she felt like a miserable fraud.

A whisper close to her ear, 'The truck cost twice as much as this car. It was a top-of-the-line Mercedes. You didn't seem uncomfortable in that.'

She turned to him in wonder. 'It looked all beaten up.'

His brows lifted. 'Drawing attention to myself wasn't the point. Staying safe in a strong ride was the sole reason I bought it. I enjoyed taking off all the strips that showed its maker, and making it look so old. Taking a hammer to the panels and scratching the duco to—what was it? Billy-o?—was really fun.'

Her mouth twitched.

'I suppose there are hammers and chisels, and sandpaper, somewhere at home,' he mused. 'I'll have to check out the cellars, or ask the carpenter.'

She frowned, tilting her head in wordless question.

He shrugged. 'If you're only going to be comfortable with who I am if you only see me as a normal man when my ride looks broken down, and I'm covered in mud and bruises, I'll have to make the arrangements.'

The coolness in the words made her flush. 'You make me sound like a snob.'

Another half-shrug. 'It isn't me doing the judging, is it? It isn't me not giving you a chance, or saying you're not good enough.'

She gasped. 'I never said you weren't good enough!'

'No, you said *you* weren't. You judge yourself—but you *have* judged me. You tell me what I need in my life when I don't even know what my future's going to be yet.'

Hana blinked, opened her mouth and closed it. He'd dissected her again—but once more, he was right. Innate honesty demanded she stop arguing, so she turned and looked out again— and saw people pointing at the crest on the doors of the saloon, speculating…waving…

'I've got a present for you.'

Startled, she turned to him. She said, hard and flat, 'I don't want it.'

A tiny smile played around the corners of his mouth. 'Don't judge my gift before you see it.' He handed her a gorgeously wrapped box, tied with a golden ribbon. 'Just open it, Hana, before you judge me or what I've given.'

Shamed by the reminder, she kept her eyes on the box as she untied the ribbon and opened it—and burst into startled laughter. Inside the intricately crafted sandalwood box lay a card saying 'Hana's Emergency Escape Kit.' Beneath that were a few dozen energy bars, four canteens…and two little dropper bottles of lavender.

She looked up at him, still laughing. 'Um, thank you?'

He leaned forward and brushed his mouth over hers. 'I accept that some time soon you're going to want to run, my star. But as the song says, if you leave me, can I come too?'

Huskily, knowing it was a pipe dream, she murmured, 'I'd like that.'

'We're going to be okay, Sahar Thurayya.' He kissed her again. 'Souls entwined bring us greater strength than one alone.'

The shining happiness in his eyes lodged her breath in her throat. She touched his hand. 'Thank you. Thank you for accepting me as I am.'

Then she saw they'd already swept through the two sets of ornate, protective gates, and were at the private rear entrance of the palace.

Suddenly she understood what he'd done for her. He'd taken her mind from her family just when she couldn't stand *thinking* about them any more. He'd planned the gift before she'd even agreed to come, knowing she'd need her mind turned from the turmoil within.

'Thank you for distracting me,' she murmured, her stomach filled with bats without sonar, crashing around inside her; but she turned to him and, before she could chicken out, leaned into him and kissed his mouth. 'You're a truly good man, Alim El-Kanar.'

His eyes, dark with emotion as she kissed him, turned bleak. 'I wish I could believe that.' The moment the car stopped he was out, not waiting for a servant to open it and hand him out as custom demanded. He waved the servant away, and turned to help her. 'Your family's waiting inside, in an antechamber to the left.'

Her legs turned to jelly and she wanted to throw up. She clung to his hand, just trying to breathe. 'Come with me. Please,' she whispered.

He led her up the wide marble stairs and through the gold-lined oak doors. 'I can't stay beyond introductions. Unfortunately, I have my own ghosts to face.' Swiftly his mouth brushed hers. 'We'll survive this, Hana. We can meet for recon after.' He showed her to the wide double doors where her family waited, and led her inside.

Five people on luxurious woven settees jumped to their feet the moment the doors opened. Five people dressed in their best, either for her or to impress Alim, she didn't know. People who'd once meant the world to her—and her heart jerked, as if telling her what she wanted to forget: they still meant so much…too much.

'Hana,' her mother murmured, voice cracking with emotion. Her plump, comfortable frame had lessened; her face was lined, her eyes weary and filled with tears. A hand reached out to Hana, and hovered there, as if asking a question her mouth couldn't ask.

'Hello, Mum,' she greeted her mother in stilted English, bowing her head. The word fell from her lips, rusted with disuse. She kept her hands by her sides: keeping a distance for the sake of safety. The last time she'd seen her mother, she'd been wringing her hands and asking why, *why* hadn't she come to her mother and *said* she wanted Mukhtar instead of Latif...

She couldn't look at her father—then she couldn't *not* look at him. A flicked glance— enough to see the painful guilt and eagerness to make amends—and she looked away. 'Amal and Malik Al-Sud, this is...' Now her uncertain gaze swung to Alim, taking in the utter opulence of the white-and-gold room as she turned. How did she introduce him?

'Alim El-Kanar,' Alim went on so smoothly it was as if he were on the other side of a mirror from her, able to finish her sentences. He moved forward, hand extended to her father. 'I'm very pleased to meet you. You've raised a daughter of amazing strength and courage.'

After the men gripped hands to the elbow, a custom of respect here, and Alim bowed to her mother, there was an awkward moment. 'Hana,' her mother said again, taking a step forward.

Hana closed her eyes, shook her head. She didn't want contact. *Who sees how alone you are in your strength?* She'd given her time, strength and self away, but no one but Alim had held her, comforted her in years; she'd been alone.

A hand rested on her shoulder, warm and strong. Alim. 'Were you given coffee?' he asked, giving her time, space from the emotion.

She wanted to rest back against him, to lay her hand over his and thank him for again coming to her rescue. How well he knew her, even when she'd done her best to lock him out—and she knew then that his accusation in the jet had been a hollow drum, a distraction for her sake: her heart was laid bare for him to see.

'Yes, thank you, my lord.' Her father's voice, the first words of his she'd heard since that fateful night. *You will marry Mukhtar, Hana, for your sister's sake. It's not Fatima's fault you couldn't control your passions!*

'I can't do this. I—I have to—' Hana whirled for the door.

'Hana, don't go. Please. We love you. We've missed you so much.'

Fatima's voice, choked up. Hana stopped as if frozen in place. Slowly, her hands curled into fists. 'At least you all had each other.' Flat words, locking her sister out; she had no alternative unless she wanted to cry like a baby. 'I hope you had a lovely wedding, Fatima. Better than mine was…or so I hear mine was. I missed the party.' She turned, looked at her father for a moment, saw the anguish. 'Perhaps we can have a family celebration of the annulment. I'd really like to be there to celebrate one major event in my life.'

Another stretch of silence that felt like dead calm water after a long storm, and she felt their pain as clearly as her own, and she tried to strengthen herself, to harden her heart. She felt close to breaking…

'You're thinner.' Her mother's voice quivered.

Still she couldn't turn around, or look at them. 'Rather hard to get enough to eat at times,' she said, light and shadow together. 'You either toughen up or fall apart in the Sahel.'

'You served in the Sahel,' Fatima said, her voice faint. 'It's the most dangerous place on earth…'

Hana shrugged. 'As I said, you get tough when just finding enough to eat each day is the greatest challenge facing you. It makes other problems, like being forced into marriage with a drug runner, seem…insignificant.'

'Excuse me, please. I have to meet my brother,' Alim said quietly, and left the massive room, closing the doors behind him.

Hana watched him go, and hated him for leaving her here with these people…her family, half strangers now, just people she'd once known.

'You saved his life,' her brother Khalid muttered, shaking his head. 'My little sister saved our sheikh and brought him back to his people.'

She shrugged, and didn't answer. In this place, talking about Alim seemed too hard.

'You are being touted as a national heroine,' her mother said, shaky, emotional. Again her hand lifted, reached out to her.

Hana stepped back, aching, angry. 'That'll only last until the media finds out about Mukhtar. Then I'll be a national disgrace, won't I? Will you disown me then, too?'

'Hana, please.' Her father spoke, his voice pleading. 'I know what I've done to you. When Mukhtar was arrested, and we knew you spoke the truth, I looked for you—'

'Oh, only then?' she asked lightly. 'You didn't try to find me before, force me back to my lawful master to spare you all any more family embarrassment? How long did it take you to work out that I didn't lie to you, that I couldn't possibly have slept with my fiancé's brother?'

Her oldest sister Tanihah said quietly, 'Hana, it's over now, we know the woman you are. Now you're back with us, where you belong. Can't we move past this?'

'I belong nowhere.' Hana shook her head. *Just don't cry, don't cry...* 'There's nowhere to move to. You can't possibly understand what it's like to live as I have the past five years.' Always running, terrified of being forced into Mukhtar's bed— 'The damage is done, Tanihah.' Saying her sister's name—they'd once been so close— broke her. 'I have to go.'

She ran to the door, yanked it open, and fled through into the main entrance, heading with unerring instinct for the nearest escape.

A burly guard blocked the way. 'Miss al-Sud, my lord Sheikh has asked that you await him in his private chamber when your meeting was over.'

The look on the man's face—calm, implacable—told her there was no way out. Alim had anticipated her escape, and made certain she couldn't outrun her ghosts. She lifted her chin, nodded and followed the man to another room, knowing her family watched her through the open doors. She felt their hunger, their pain—the guilt eating at them.

Yet if it weren't for what had happened, she'd never have met Alim…

With all her heart she yearned to go back in that room, to tell them it was all right, she forgave them, would be part of the family circle again. But the circle had fractured five years before, and, even if she could make peace, the cracks in the join would always show.

The damage is done.

'Welcome home, Alim,' Amber said in her quiet way. Alim felt the repressed emotion beneath. 'It's good to have you back.'

Is it? He smiled and played the game with his beautiful, cold sister-in-law. Truth was vulgar. Sweep all the dirt under the carpet and believe it never happened. 'Thank you, Amber.'

This room had been Fadi's reception room where he met foreign dignitaries. Alim had thought it would be too hard to be here, to see the reminders, but Hana's painful reunion had somehow changed things for him. He felt warm, comforted by the memories…and if he still hadn't forgiven himself for his part in Fadi's death, and maybe never would, he knew it was time to come back to stay—and Fadi wouldn't want it any other way. Fadi would always have wanted him to do his duty, and care for their people as they'd shared the care for their little brother…

He saw Harun watching his wife, cautious, reserved—his pride hiding the hunger only his big brother would know. Harun noticed Alim watching him, and said—they'd done the emotional thirty seconds when Sh'ellah released him—'I've moved out of your room. It's ready for you, as is your office, as soon as you want to resume your duties.'

Alim felt the savagery repressed inside his brother, a seething cauldron of resentment beneath. 'Let's not pretend. Don't talk as if I've been sick for a few weeks. I was gone for years, and left all the grief and duty to you. Harun…'

His brother shrugged with eloquent understatement. 'It wasn't so bad.'

Wasn't it? He saw the distance between husband and wife, lying there like all the arid wasteland of the Sahel. 'I wanted to say, the choice is yours now. You've done a magnificent job of running the country, of picking up the pieces after Fadi's death and my disappearance. If you want to remain the sheikh—'

'*No.*'

The snarl took him by surprise—because it came from both Harun and Amber. He took the easier option, looking at Amber. Sure that her reasons would be easier to hear than Harun's.

She flushed, and glanced at Harun; fiddled with her hands, shuffled a foot, and burst out, 'I won't play sheikh's happy wife for anyone's sake. I'm tired of the pretence that everything's all right. I don't care what my father wants any more. I want a divorce.'

She turned and walked out of the room with regal grace, as if she hadn't just thrown a live bomb between the brothers.

Stunned, Alim could hardly bear to look at Harun, but when he did he saw Harun had been waiting for him to turn; his brother didn't even look surprised. 'And that's why I said no,' he said quietly. 'I'm also tired of pretending everything's all right. I've been standing in your place since long before Fadi died, helping him run the country while you were off playing the glamorous racing star, and again when you took off to play the hero. I've had ten years of living your life for you, Alim, including the wife who wanted you, not me. I've left everything you need to know in your office. I want my own life. The country's yours, brother.'

Harun followed in his wife's wake, leaving Alim to face the consequences of ten years of loving and respecting his brother without truly seeing him. 'Fadi, where are you?' he muttered, and rubbed his temples. The welcome home for the prodigal brother was far from what he'd hoped.

As he entered his office where she waited for him, one look at Alim's face told Hana his meeting had been as devastating for him as hers had been for her. The blank, dark eyes, the lost misery melted her heart; his need was hers.

She walked into his arms, holding him close. 'That bad?'

He nuzzled her hair with his lips. 'Probably worse. You?'

'Horrible,' she whispered, and shuddered.

'Harun and Amber are separating. Harun expects me to begin my duties immediately.'

She hugged him, wordless comfort—what

could she say? 'My family wants me to move past it and forgive them, and be a family again.'

'They expect us to behave as if all these years never happened.' There was a curious note in his voice. 'For me, that's only what I deserve. But you…'

She held him closer. 'I want to forgive them, Alim. I just can't look at them…'

Softly, he said, 'Then maybe you should close your eyes and say it, really fast—and see how you feel when it's out.'

'I—' Hana blinked and stared up at him, awed. 'That just might work.' She grabbed him by the hand and strode into the room where her family still waited; they knew her, knew she couldn't hold out against them for long, no matter what they'd done.

'Hana, my darling, if you'll just listen—'

She lifted a shaking hand to stop her mother's rush of words, trying to make better what would never be truly mended. She closed her eyes and said, hard and fast while clinging to Alim's hand, 'I forgive you. I want to be part of the family again, but I don't want to be rushed. Don't crowd me and don't expect me to hug you and act like everything's fine.'

A stifled sound from her mother was drowned out by her father's voice. 'We understand, *nuur il-'en*. If you will try to find true forgiveness in your heart one day, we can wait.'

Nuur il-'en: light of my eyes. Her father hadn't called her that since the day Mukhtar—

Suddenly her breaths caught over and over until she was wheezing and hiccupping at once, and she couldn't do anything but gulp while tears flowed unchecked, and broken words poured from her. 'You thought I could cheat on Latif within weeks of the engagement, hurt you all, and risk my little sister's future. You believed a stranger over your own daughter. You sacrificed me for Fatima's sake, when I'd done nothing wrong. Why, *why* did you believe him, *why*?'

After a moment, her father said, simple and sad, 'You have so much inside your heart to give, *nuur il-'en*. We always knew that when you gave your heart, it would be for life—but you didn't give your heart to Latif. You merely liked him. You only agreed to marry him to please everyone. Then Mukhtar came along, and he was ten years younger, handsome and charming. We didn't believe it at first—not until Latif said he'd always known you didn't love him, and you and

Mukhtar seemed to get on so well, always laughing and joking.'

Hana stilled at the innate truth she hadn't wanted to hear. *She hadn't loved Latif.* She'd been willing to cheat him of a real, loving wife because she'd wanted to make everyone happy. And, yes, she had found Mukhtar a fun companion at first, until she saw the real person beneath the surface charm. That was why Mukhtar had been so convincing.

Then her father's words slammed inside her soul like iron doors clanging. *When you gave your heart, it would be for life.*

Strong arms around her waist held her up when her knees shook. She turned into Alim's warm, strong body, trying to gain composure, but she couldn't stop crying. Since she'd met him all the emotion she'd stored deep inside her heart had begun flowing, and something deep inside told her she couldn't find that safe place of distance ever again. She'd given her heart to Alim and would never have it back. She'd spend her life yearning for a man she couldn't have…

'My lord, you and our daughter seem very close,' Hana's mother said quietly.

Alim felt Amal al-Sud's gaze on him, searching. In fact all five members of Hana's family were staring at him. Hana moved as if to leave his arms, but he held her there. 'Yes, we are.' He made no apology for it.

'You both must have gone through a life-changing experience,' Hana's brother Khalid said in a thoughtful tone, 'but, my lord, you know…'

'You're aware we're ordinary people,' her father finished the sentence for his son, 'and our daughter's happiness is more precious to us now than ever.'

'I want her happiness, too, because that's what she's brought to me.' He thought of the meaning of her name, and smiled at Malik al-Sud. 'I've already asked her to marry me, sir.'

'Ordered me, you mean,' the cheeky mumble came from the depths of his chest, but loud enough to make the entire family gasp.

He chuckled, and caressed her hair. 'She's right, I did—and I will marry her.' He smiled down at Hana, knowing the effect it had on her. 'Just as soon as she says yes.'

CHAPTER TWELVE

'YOU can't marry her,' Malik al-Sud said, his tone deferential yet firm. It reminded Alim of Hana. 'This is impossible—it's a fantasy based on her saving your life, my lord. The country won't accept her as your wife.'

'That's what I've been telling him,' Hana said, for once in sync with her father.

'It's only been a few weeks. You can't know if it's real, what you want, what you're feeling,' her mother added.

Her brother and sisters nodded in agreement. Alim saw the same disbelief in six pairs of eyes…especially in Hana's. Fury filled him at her lack of faith in him, but he controlled it. 'If you won't believe in us, Sahar Thurayya, then I'll have to believe for both of us—because I am going to marry you.' He bent and kissed her, feeling the little catch of breath in reaction, the tiny purr in her throat.

He lifted his head and smiled at Malik al-Sud, seeing the fire in the older man's eyes.

He frowned and shook his head, an infinitesimal movement Hana wouldn't feel. He wasn't going to answer the unasked suspicion, and hurt Hana over again. Even now, her family should know her better.

'You've raised a fine, principled woman, sir,' he said quietly, 'a woman who's a queen in every way but birth…and if she doesn't marry me, the people will have to be content with my brother as my heir, because I won't marry.'

Dead silence met his pronouncement—then Hana moved out of his arms. 'I told you, Alim, this is ridiculous. You think you love me, but you haven't been home a day. And I—I told you what kind of man I wanted…' But the telltale hiccup gave her away.

He shook his head. 'When you gave your heart, it would be for life,' he repeated her father's words in strong deliberation. 'You gave it to me, Hana. You said the words.'

Her eyes were cold, bleak. 'That was before we arrived here.' She waved at all the opulence he took for granted after all these years, because this was home. 'I grew up in a house the size of this room. I caught buses and trains when I wanted to go somewhere. I'm more Australian than Arabic in many ways. It isn't just about the people's reaction, Alim, or the press. I—I do care for you, but this life isn't what I want!'

Looking in her eyes, he saw the absolute sincerity—and something died inside him. 'You mean that.'

He heard the doors closing behind her family.

Hana's eyes were drenched in tears, lovely pools of green-brown finality. 'I've spent five years in huts and camps, working with people who have nothing. This—' She shook her head. 'I can't be what I'm not, Alim. I couldn't live this way, not when friends, people I love…'

Strange, but coming here today, he hadn't thought about how his childhood home would affect a woman who'd lived with death by starvation every day of the past five years. He'd been too busy thinking of their families, of making her see they were meant to be together. Coming here, he'd finally made peace with Fadi's death, come to terms with his future, and the only question that remained in his mind had been when Hana would marry him.

Now, without even looking around, he saw the palace through Hana's eyes—the gold lining the walls, the knick-knacks worth thousands and millions, meant to impress dignitaries who'd been there, done that a hundred times, in every other nation—

He saw in his mind's eye the multimillion-dollar cheques for racing a million-dollar car around a circuit…the oil that had turned his country from a rural backwater barely known outside the emirates to a world player. Riches, power, and the trappings of wealth everywhere…he saw all his life's achievements through her eyes.

Then he saw the people of Shellah-Akbar risking their lives to save him, people lean with hunger and bent with long hours of hard physical labour every day. He saw Hana in her burq'a, her capable hands saving his life, her sacrifices for his sake.

He was trapped here, unless he lumbered everything back on Harun's shoulders—and as Hana had said, he'd had one shot at disappearing. He couldn't do it again. He could offer to give it all away to please her, to save others, and still it wouldn't be enough.

For the first time in his life, Alim was speechless.

'I think it's best if I go to my sister's house,' she said quietly, breaking into his inner darkness, but not lightening it as she'd always done before. She knew.

'You're running again.' He felt his jaw tightening. 'You can go anywhere in the world, you can escape again, do the noble thing and return to the life we lived before. But it will always be running away from the hard option.'

Her gaze turned from him. 'I know,' she mumbled.

He brought her back to face him. 'I might not have a choice any more, but inside I'm still the guy in the truck. This isn't the life you think it is. Yes, I live in luxury, but being the leader of any country is as hard as anything you've done in the Sahel in many ways—and from now on, it'll be harder, Hana. I'll be working for those I now know.'

Her eyes glimmered softly, tears and pride combined. 'I know that, Alim. You're a truly good man.'

It was a farewell he refused to believe. 'My job would be easier if I had someone beside me. A woman who knows and understands the common people—who's lived the life of those who suffer the most. A permanent reminder for me never to forget, or to become arrogant.' He kissed her again. 'You can take the hard option or the easy one, Hana. Save a few with your hands, or save hundreds of thousands with your courage and great heart. You can take on a new job with a real challenge, working night and day for the good of so many more at a time than one village alone.'

He saw the doubt in her heart, the uncertainty in her eyes, and had to be satisfied with that. 'I'll be here, waiting,' he said, a soft growl.

'Don't. Don't wait for me, Alim.' Her voice cracked. 'Thanks for the escape kit. Thank you—for everything.'

And she was gone.

'Thank you,' he said softly to the air she'd left behind. He breathed in lavender—she must have put on some from the bottle he'd given her—and felt aching loss.

As she'd predicted, the world media didn't take long to dig up her story—and Hana became a celebrity and disgrace at once.

Sheikh's Saviour is a Drug Runner's Ex-wife!

She didn't have to read the papers to know that

all she'd done through the years counted for nothing. Even saving Alim's life meant less than the scandal they could create to sell papers. They found Mukhtar and called the prison for his point of view. They found out about Latif, and, though Latif refused to comment, they ran the whole sordid story as they saw it, and speculated on her relationship with Alim.

Sex sells.

She wanted to laugh and cry at once. Such exquisite irony: the virgin who'd slept with two brothers at once, and seduced a sheikh. What would she do next?

Alim had taken up his duties with a vengeance. According to the papers, he'd had the villagers resettled in the countryside west of Sar Abbas, the capital, and gave them land with water and all they needed to restart their lives. He'd given a speech on his life the past three years. The passion in his words as he spoke of life in the Sahel, as relayed on TV, brought such longing to her heart she couldn't speak, couldn't move. Oh, how she loved him…

He was creating a foundation for the forgotten people, calling for funds to send engineers and geologists to find water, to buy generators and pumps so every village could have a water source. He talked about his time in captivity, and how he hated that his ransom would create a further cycle of misery for the innocent.

Alim was as good as his word. He was using his position to help others. Taking the hard road and making something of it in a way one single nurse in a village never could.

For the first time in years Hana knew how it felt to be trapped physically. She was holed up in her sister's house with hundreds of people outside, and she couldn't hide. She couldn't run to the next place, and put her fears and her misery behind her. She couldn't run from her family when they wanted to talk, to get close, to ask her about Alim.

For the first time in years, she had to deal with her feelings instead of hiding behind others' problems, using them to ignore her own, or to feel good about herself and her sacrifices. *My Hana, always needing to be the strong one, the clever one, the fastest and the best. When will you learn to love yourself, and know that all you need to be loved is just to be yourself?*

Fourteen-year-old words of wisdom had finally caught up with her. Stuck in Tanihah's house there were no excuses any more. She couldn't hide behind her grades or her job or her burq'a, her family's betrayal or her lower position in life. The mirror she'd outrun for so many years was being held right up to her face, and she was the one holding it.

Alim was right: she was a coward, and no matter how dangerous a place she went to next or how many lives she saved, she was still a frightened child trying to prove she was strong. She'd chosen Latif for safety; she'd run from Mukhtar—and she was running from Alim, using birth and a lie to keep herself at a safe distance from him. But this time it hadn't helped; she loved him more every day, ached for him, and struggled against the knowledge that the only thing keeping them apart was her fear.

When you give your heart, it will be for life...

Almost two weeks after the story hit the news she sat in her niece's room, on the bed she shared with Atiya, needing space and quiet. When night fell, and they'd finished prayer—Ramadan had begun, and eating in the hours of sunlight was forbidden unless you were a child—she came to eat with the family, and answered their questions at random, giving them stark honesty but not even knowing she did. The doorbell had stopped ringing at last, but the sharks were surrounding the house still, hoping for some juicy gossip. Hana barely noticed that either. Totally lost in the self-knowledge she'd avoided all her life. Thin delusions, as she'd said to Alim, were stripped away and she saw the person she was.

To her shock, she didn't hate herself as much as she'd feared. She was a coward, but one who'd saved lives. Yes, she ran from emotion when it became too hard, but now she was facing the hardest emotions of her life, she was okay. She hid behind her position, behind Alim's position so she didn't have to say, *Yes, I'll stop running and I'll marry you—*

And to change that one, she'd have to face Alim again.

And do what? she asked herself wearily. There was no getting around the facts as presented by the media—her birth wasn't and never would be good enough, her fake marriage put Alim way out of her reach—unless she could make the changes herself.

If you won't marry me, I'll live alone.

I'm thirty-seven, not a boy. I know what I want. I want you.

I'll be here waiting.

It came to this: she could be a safe, lonely coward for the rest of her life, or she could finally *live*. Live with the man she loved, and make a difference to the world.

She waited for a lull in the family dinner conversation, and threw her bomb. 'I want to tell the media the truth. All of it, about Mukhtar and why I was in the Sahel.'

They all turned to stare at her, even the children at the small table.

She held her father's unfathomable gaze with one of her own. 'I love Alim,' she said, and it felt amazingly good to have it out there. 'I want a future with him.'

'It won't happen while the people believe the worst,' her father agreed, still with that Sphinx-like face.

Her mother said in a muffled voice, 'Many don't believe the worst, Hana. The letters to the editor are overwhelmingly in your favour.'

She hesitated, but decided to say it. 'It will embarrass the family, make you look bad.'

Her dad's eyes swept the table and everyone on it. 'I made choices I believe others will understand—and if they don't, then it's a judgement I deserve.' He pushed back his chair. 'This is my responsibility.'

'Dad…' she mumbled, using the loving title for the first time since returning.

He smiled at her. 'You need to find that man of yours and tell him how you feel. Leave the story to me. Trust me, *nuur il-'en*. I won't let you down this time.'

With tears in her eyes, she too stood, walked around to her father and touched his arm: the closest she'd voluntarily come to him in five years. 'Thank you, Dad.'

There was only one way. She called the number on the card Alim's driver had given her—Alim's private number. 'Hi. It's me. I'm stuck in my sister's house, surrounded by the media. Can you send a car for me, with some men to help me through the crowd?'

'Of course.' Alim's voice was reserved, so tired. 'Do you need anything more?'

'I need to see you. We need to talk.' She gulped and coughed to clear the thickness in her throat. 'Can I come to you?'

'I'll come to you.'

'The house is surrounded, Alim. In the palace they can't get to us, or put cameras through the windows. Tell the guards to come to the back door and knock four times.'

'All right, then. I'll be waiting for you in my private study.' He sounded so neutral…

What more did she deserve? But now, this night, she wasn't giving in to fear again. This wasn't about protecting herself from pain. She'd done that for too many years, and had only emptiness as her reward. She hung up and raced for the shower…

Fifteen minutes later, she was ready when a knock came at the back door. She opened it, and two burly, exquisitely dressed guards ushered her down the stairs and around the front. The press, all avidly listening to her father, made a dash for her as she ran to the saloon car, but the guards yelled, 'Miss al-Sud has no comment,' and elbowed any intrepid reporter out of the way.

The trip to the palace was followed by a dozen cars, and a few racing motorbikes with photographers snapping pictures of her.

The gates opened. The car drove around the back. The guards handed her out and raced her up the stairs, inside and to the left.

They opened the doors for her, and in another exquisite room, quietly appointed in cherrywood and strong masculine pieces, Alim stood by the empty fireplace, his forehead resting on his hand. 'Hi,' she said when the guards closed the door behind her.

He didn't look up, didn't turn to her. 'Hi.'

He sounded so unutterably weary, her heart jerked. 'A rough few days?'

'A rough few weeks,' he agreed. 'I'm exhausted, Hana, so let's get this over with.'

For the first time since their rescue, he wasn't opening his heart to her. He was expecting a kiss-off…or maybe he wanted one.

I will not run. I won't be a coward again! Alim deserved to know how she felt.

But as she drew close to him she chickened out. 'I thought you should know Dad's with the press now, telling the true story, about Mukhtar, Latif and me…and you.' She took a step to him, and another, her heart aching.

'My press secretary told me. It's already on the TV,' Alim said on a sigh. 'That's good of your father. Your name's being cleared. They'll all love you again.'

'But that wasn't why I came,' she blurted out, angry with herself for being so weak. 'I came to say…to say…' She sighed in self-fury, and closed her eyes and said whatever came to her head. 'I can't do this any more, Alim. I can't lie to myself and pretend—'

'Pretend what, Hana?' he asked, his voice hard and ragged at once. 'While you've been hiding out with your family to support you, I've been facing the press, the people, learning the job over again. Harun and Amber left the same day you did. He's gone incommunicado and left me with everything. I'm doing it alone, barely getting three hours' sleep a night, so can we get this over with?'

She blinked at him…but saw in his words the blunt honesty of a man on the edge of falling down. A man who desperately needed her but wouldn't say it. Expecting her to run again and refusing to fight any longer. He accepted her as she was, even now…

At that, Hana forgot her needs and fears, and ran to him. She put down the box she'd brought on the desk beside them, and took him into her arms. 'You're not alone. I'm here,' she whispered, kissing his cheek, holding him—and it felt so good to be giving, this time in honesty. 'I came to give you something.'

'Do I want it?' he muttered into her hair, holding onto her as if she were a lifeline, breathing in deeply, and she was glad she'd put on the lavender again.

She smiled. 'I hope so.' Reaching behind her, she brought the box to him. 'Open it.'

He looked down at the sandalwood box he'd given her in the car weeks before. 'Why…?'

'Just open it,' she insisted softly. She couldn't wait much longer.

He opened the box. On top of the emergency escape kit he'd given her was her burq'a. He stared at the contents, then looked up at her, his eyes hollow with exhaustion. There was a question there.

'Read the note,' she said quietly.

He found it beneath the burq'a. *Hana cannot run without these*. And he looked at her again. Either he wasn't getting it, or he wanted her to say it.

She reached up and kissed those poor, tired eyes, one by one. 'I'm giving them to you. I'm entrusting you with my treasures, Alim. I won't run without them, and I don't want to run without you. You're my peace, my best friend, my love. If you can't disappear when the going gets tough, neither will I.' She held his face in her hands and said, 'I won't be a coward any more. I love you, Alim, and whatever you need me to be—whatever the country will allow me to be for you—I'll be it.'

With a swift movement, he tossed the box in a far corner. 'Hana,' he said hoarsely, turning her face and kissing her mouth like a man parched. 'My star, you'd better mean this, because I'll never give you this box back. I'll never let you go again.'

'Good,' she said, intense with all the emotion she'd kept from him all this time, giving him everything but the one thing he'd needed: *herself*. Now she was open to him at last, and she'd never hide from him again. 'I need you so much, Alim. I need to be beside you every day of my life. If the people won't let us marry—'

He pulled back to grin at her. He looked haggard, hollow-eyed, and so happy she knew she'd never be a coward again. The rewards for true courage were perfect and life-changing. 'You haven't been reading the papers, have you? There's been a huge backlash against the stories about you. The people know I'd never have come back but for you. You saved my life and gave me back to them. That's far more important to them than any bloodline.' His eyes darkened. 'But if the whole country was against us I'd still marry you, Sahar Thurayya. They might need me, but I need you.'

'And I need you. I love you so much.' She melted against him. 'I really need you to kiss me,' she murmured, reaching up to bring him down to her.

The long, frantic kiss was everything she'd dreamed of in the longest two weeks of her life without him; being close to him, feeling his love for her—

'I've been going insane without you,' he whispered between kisses. 'I thought you'd never come back, that I had nothing to offer you that would make you stay.'

She kissed him again and again. 'You,' she mumbled back. 'You're all I need—and to be needed, Alim. Seeing you on TV, how strong and brave you are but so alone…'

'You'll take the job?' he asked, moulding her body along his, as if making an imprint of her on him. 'It's not an easy place to be, Sahar Thurayya. But we can change the world from here. We can help make things better.'

'An irresistible offer to a control freak like me,' she laughed, and kissed him again. 'But I warn you, my love, I won't be your common, garden variety queen.' *Me, a queen,* she thought in wonder. Was she in a fairy tale, or dreaming? But

Alim felt so wonderfully real against her, the desire filling her so perfect… 'You know I won't bend to the rules all the time, and will break them half the time.'

He chuckled, and another long kiss followed. 'Think I don't know that? I know you, my star— and I happen to think rattling some cages will be good for the stick-in-the-muds. I intend rattling more than a few cages myself.'

The doors burst open after a quick knock. 'My lord, there's something you need to see—' The man goggled at the sight of his ruler locked in an embrace with the woman who'd saved his life, and began backing out of the room with profuse, mumbled apologies.

Alim said coolly, 'Put everything on hold unless it's national emergency, Ratib. I'm spending quality time with my wife-to-be.'

'Yes, of course, my lord…' The doors closed.

He winked at her. 'Ten, nine, eight…and the whole palace knows.' And from behind him, in a drawer in the desk, he brought out a long, wide, dark-red velvet box and opened it. 'Your engagement present,' he said gently. 'When my mother knew she was dying, she chose these for my future bride, hoping she'd like diamonds. I've kept it with me like a talisman the past few weeks, trying to believe you'd come back to me.'

Hana gasped, staring down at the rose-gold ring with a dazzling diamond solitaire, with bracelets, earrings and a necklace to match. 'Oh…oh, Alim…'

Alim took her left hand from his shoulder, and, with a smile, slid the ring onto her finger—he'd had it resized with the help of Hana's parents, with whom he'd been in daily contact. 'At last,' he growled softly, and leaned to do something he'd fantasised about through the long, lonely weeks without her: nibble on her ear. 'No more doubts. No running away.'

'Never,' she breathed, her face alight and shining with desire and love. He kissed the pulse-point behind her jaw and her head fell back, her face flushed and her chest rose and fell with breaths of growing passion. 'Alim, I love you, I want you so much. Don't make me wait for a massive wedding,' she cried, her voice throbbing with desire.

He'd come a long way from the man who believed no woman could want him—but when he nuzzled her neck, he revelled in the way her body quivered against him. Then he drew back, his face holding the rueful acceptance in his heart. 'We have little choice in the waiting, my star. You're going to be a ruler's wife, the equivalent of a queen. The people will expect to share in the full, traditional courtship. We also have to coordinate a time that the Heads of State who wish to come will be able to attend. We can't offend anyone. It'll take at least four to six months.'

Her eyes closed hard; her lips pressed together. 'I thought you'd say that,' she whispered glumly, 'but, oh, it's going to be so hard, waiting months for you. I want you *now*.' She buried her blushing face in his chest. 'I'm sorry, I know I'm not the traditional view of what I should be, but I can't help it. I love you, I want you so much.'

She spoke of the ancient tradition where a woman must fight her man against his taking her to prove her innocence and chastity, a woman worth keeping...but Alim already knew that and more about his brave, lovely dawn star. She'd healed him heart and soul, made him a man and a ruler again...for the first time in his life, he truly felt whole. He smiled, moved by the depth of her love for him. 'And never was a tradition broken that means more to me,' he replied, kissing her nose, her mouth. 'Nothing about us has followed tradition, my star, but for a little while, now, we have to. It's important that the people see our courtship as pure and honourable.'

He heard her gulp. 'All right...then we shouldn't be alone at any time until we're married, because all you have to do is touch me, and I quiver and ache with need for you.' She held him hard as his mind blanked out with the intensity of his happiness. 'I didn't mean that I don't want to see you. I want to be with you all the time, but when I am, all I want is to touch you. And when I touch you, all I want is to make love with you.'

How could he not love, adore this woman? He lifted her face to his. 'Hana, your parents named you perfectly, because you are my happiness.'

She smiled up at him. 'And your parents were right, too, because you've been so wise in everything you've done for me, and in waiting for me.' She went up on her toes to kiss him again and again. 'I want to be by your side every day, every night for the rest of my life.'

'You will be,' he murmured as he turned her around to clasp the diamond necklace around her throat, the bracelet around her wrist: the traditional signs of a bridegroom who cherished his wife-to-be. As he placed the gold and amber veil of the engaged woman on her head, the final part of his first engagement gift to her, he murmured again, 'You will be.'

EPILOGUE

Eight years later

'SHE'S all scrunched and wrinkly,' four-year-old Tariq pronounced. He was looking down at his only sister, born the night before, with a touch of distaste.

'She's supposed to be, silly. Babies are all ugly—but she'll get prettier, and you're still ugly,' their oldest, six-and-a-half-year-old Fadi, said, shoving at his little brother with an open palm. Tariq responded with a shove back, setting off their youngest son Sami, making the two-year-old wail in indignation.

'Boys, boys, Mama's too tired for this—and you'll wake Johara,' Alim reproved his sons, but with an indulgent air as he gathered their youngest son in his arms to comfort him.

Having their children with them every single

day, all the time when they weren't immersed in affairs of state, was a tradition Hana had begun with Fadi's birth. She'd refused every argument against breast-feeding her children, and insisted on both parents seeing their children for at least a few hours every day—she called it playtime. The family also ate together on every night there were no visitors of state.

With the boys being natural children who knew how to behave—well, mostly, but their occasional childish outbursts made people laugh more than they censured—almost everyone in the nation was convinced of his wife's wisdom. The initial resistance to their marriage, in the more traditional, old-fashioned sector of the nation, soon faded when they saw how much Hana loved him. The people loved Hana for being one of them, remembering her roots and being proud of them. Alim loved that his children felt free to climb on his lap or come to him for a cuddle instead of their nanny or tutor when they were tired or had hurt themselves. His children were completely themselves, felt free to laugh or play or yell when the family were alone…and they knew they were loved by their parents.

And Alim knew his wife utterly adored him.

Hana had taken months of lessons in royal deportment, but they hadn't lasted long. She'd completely failed at royal reserve in public; she spoke her mind, and the people loved her for being their advocate against highborn self-interest.

They also loved her for not being able to hide that she loved her husband to distraction.

His two oldest sons kept fighting until Alim put up his hand. 'I said Mama's tired. Fadi, you're old enough to control yourself for your mother's sake. She's in pain.'

Fadi sobered, looking anxiously at Hana. 'Did you hurt yourself, Mama?'

Hana gave her boys a tired, loving smile. It had been a quick but painful birth for her, and as usual, she'd refused pain relief. 'It always hurts having a baby, my angel—but Johara's worth the pain. You were all worth the pain.'

Alim quickly took a sleeping Johara from his wife's arms as the boys, hearing the 'Mama needs a cuddle' note in her voice, scrambled over the bed to reach her first. Sami wailed again when he didn't win, and his older brothers staked their claim all over her; but Hana made a place for him at her breast, and he snuggled in with a happy sigh.

An hour later, when he could see Hana was struggling to keep her eyes open, Alim called for Raina, the nanny, who ushered the children out after many lingering hugs and kisses. The boys would be spending the night with Hana's parents, in the magnificent house near the palace Alim had given them as a bride gift. Hana's brother and sisters and their families were joining Malik and Amal, to celebrate Johara's birth. Harun and Amber were coming also, from wherever in the world they were now. Harun, finally free to do as he wished, had first fought for his marriage, and won Amber back. To his surprise, he'd discovered the wife he'd barely known shared his passion for ancient history—so when he'd gone back to his archaeology studies, she'd studied right alongside him. Now his little family—they were due to have their third child in about twelve weeks—roamed the world as they discovered the past together.

And Alim couldn't be happier for him.

He put his sleeping daughter in her cradle by the bed and covered her tenderly. About to leave the room—there was a mountain of work waiting in his office—he saw his wife watching him, saw the 'Hana needs a cuddle' look on her face, mentally tossed the work out the window and lay beside her on the bed, taking her into his arms. 'You okay?'

She made a small sound of contentment as she snuggled close, her head in the hollow of his shoulder. 'I am now.'

The sleepy note in her voice was infectious, and he found himself yawning too. 'Hmm, maybe I can grab a quick nap.' Though Hana had cared for the baby last night, he'd woken most times with her, changed the nappies, and could never resist holding his tiny daughter in his arms for a few minutes, just looking at her, loving her. Much as they loved their boys and wouldn't change them, they'd wanted a daughter for so long.

At his words, Hana rolled carefully over to the phone, and dialled four, to her personal assistant. 'Roula, I want no disturbances for either of us for an hour, please. My husband and I are tired. Yes, thank you.' She moved back into his arms, smiling up at him, her eyes heavy with exhausted love. 'No talking now. Johara will wake up soon enough for a feed.' She snuggled down, rolling over so he held her close.

They both loved to sleep that way. Hana said

they were like koalas—they slept spoon-shaped, one holding the other like a koala baby on its mother's back, and when one rolled over, so did the other, and they cuddled that way.

Waking or sleeping, if they were alone, if he wasn't touching her, she was touching him. They loved being together as much now as when they were newlyweds…and he knew that, even in pain now from childbirth, Hana would soon be counting the days until they could make love.

I don't want separate royal bedrooms. When we're married, I'll sleep where my husband sleeps, she'd said firmly within a week of their engagement, creating her first scandal with the unexpected pronouncement. She'd caused her second scandal soon after, when she'd constantly dragged him into cupboards and private ante-chambers to kiss him during the long months waiting for the wedding, causing staffers no end of headaches as they tried to find him. But they'd shared a room continuously since their wedding night, and she loved and cared for her family in a way few ruling wives had ever done. The children loved that she got down on the floor with them to play, to invent things, even to show them how to behave in political and social situations by using their toys and stuffed animals as heads of state.

As for Alim, he was the happiest man in the nation. His loving, unconventional wife was everything he'd always dreamed of but never thought he'd be blessed enough to find.

He'd finally found a measure of peace for his part in Fadi's death, thanks to Hana. He'd accepted the joy as well as the responsibility in his position, and found a deep, abiding happiness he'd never imagined with his family life. In return, he'd helped her grow closer to her family, to let forgiveness come from the heart. As for Alim, he loved Hana's family, and had long been grateful to them. He was even grateful to Mukhtar. If not for that episode in Hana's life, she'd be Latif's wife, and he would never have met her.

'Alim,' she murmured moments later, obviously half asleep.

Clouded in a tired haze himself, Alim stirred. 'Hmm?'

She made that happy little sound he loved. 'Nothing,' she mumbled, her arm over his, her hand holding him there. 'Just—my Alim. Mine.'

He was sliding towards sleep, a smile curving

his lips. 'Mmm-hmm. Always.' He pulled her even closer, and drifted into dreams.

They were still in the same position when their daughter woke them nearly two hours later.

* * * * *

MILLS & BOON PUBLISH EIGHT LARGE PRINT TITLES A MONTH. THESE ARE THE EIGHT TITLES FOR NOVEMBER 2010.

A NIGHT, A SECRET…A CHILD
Miranda Lee

HIS UNTAMED INNOCENT
Sara Craven

THE GREEK'S PREGNANT LOVER
Lucy Monroe

THE MÉLENDEZ FORGOTTEN MARRIAGE
Melanie Milburne

AUSTRALIA'S MOST ELIGIBLE BACHELOR
Margaret Way

THE BRIDESMAID'S SECRET
Fiona Harper

CINDERELLA: HIRED BY THE PRINCE
Marion Lennox

THE SHEIKH'S DESTINY
Melissa James

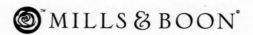

MILLS & BOON PUBLISH EIGHT LARGE PRINT TITLES A MONTH. THESE ARE THE EIGHT TITLES FOR DECEMBER 2010.

THE PREGNANCY SHOCK
Lynne Graham

FALCO: THE DARK GUARDIAN
Sandra Marton

ONE NIGHT...NINE-MONTH SCANDAL
Sarah Morgan

THE LAST KOLOVSKY PLAYBOY
Carol Marinelli

DOORSTEP TWINS
Rebecca Winters

THE COWBOY'S ADOPTED DAUGHTER
Patricia Thayer

SOS: CONVENIENT HUSBAND REQUIRED
Liz Fielding

WINNING A GROOM IN 10 DATES
Cara Colter

WEB_M&B_RTL3 LP

Discover Pure Reading Pleasure with

Visit the Mills & Boon website for all the latest in romance

Buy all the latest releases, backlist and eBooks

Find out more about our authors and their books

Join our community and chat to authors and other readers

Free online reads from your favourite authors

Win with our fantastic online competitions

Sign up for our free monthly eNewsletter

Tell us what you think by signing up to our reader panel

Rate and review books with our star system

www.millsandboon.co.uk

 Follow us at twitter.com/millsandboonuk

 Become a fan at facebook.com/romancehq

ML   11/12